P9-CKO-061

Finding Hattie

Finding Hattie

SALLY WARNER

HarperCollins*Publishers*

First, I acknowledge my debt to the following books,
which helped me prepare to write this book: Sharon Dean's
Homeward Bound, a biography of Constance Fenimore Woolson
(University of Tennessee Press, 1995); Marc McCutcheon's *The Writer's
Guide to Everyday Life in the 1800s* (Writer's Digest Books, 1993);
Emily Thornwell's *The Lady's Guide to Perfect Gentility* (1856) (The
Huntington Library and Art Gallery, 1984); and Joan Jacobs
Brumberg's *The Body Project: An Intimate History of American Girls*
(Vintage Press, 1997). I especially thank my patient and
imaginative researcher, Alexa Brandenberg, who, it turns out,
lives only a block away from Miss Bulkley's old school—
a building that is still standing. I thank my husband, Christopher
Davis, for living in the past with me for such a very long time.
Finally, I thank my great-grandmother, Hattie Knowlton Smith,
for writing a wonderful journal. All journal entries in
this novel are her own.

Finding Hattie
Copyright © 2001 by Sally Warner
Printed in the U.S.A. All rights reserved.
www.harperchildrens.com

Library of Congress Cataloging-in-Publication Data
Warner, Sally.
Finding Hattie / Sally Warner.
p.   cm.
Summary: In 1882 Hattie, a fourteen-year-old orphan, joins her cousin Sophie in
attending boarding school at Miss Bulkley's Seminary for Young Ladies in Tarrytown,
New York, and tries to find her place in the world.
ISBN 0-06-028464-1 — ISBN 0-06-028455-2 (lib. bdg.)
[1. Boarding schools—Fiction.   2. Schools—Fiction.   3. Orphans—Fiction.   4.
Cousins—Fiction.   5. Tarrytown (N.Y.)—Fiction.]   I. Title.
PZ7.W24644 Fi   2001   00-039728
[Fic]—dc21

Typography by Robbin Gourley
1   2   3   4   5   6   7   8   9   10
❖
First Edition

To the memory of my grandmother,
Julie Warner, Hattie's daughter, who took beautiful care of
old things—and of children, too

CONTENTS

Time, like an ever-rolling stream,
Bears all our years away;
They fly forgotten, as a dream
Dies at the opening day.
—Isaac Watts

NEW CLOTHES

*T*here will be no more mourning clothes for Harriet allowed in *this* household," Aunt Margaret decreed, three months following Hattie's arrival. She patted her lips with a napkin after swallowing an icy spoonful of lemon sherbet. "I think they're terribly vulgar for the young," she added with a sniff.

So this was to be a decision based upon Aunt Margaret's notion of what was fashionable. Well, I don't care, Hattie thought dully. I don't need to wear black clothing to re-member Great-Aunt Lydia and Joey. Hattie clenched the white damask napkin in her lap, though; it creased and almost crackled under its layer of starch.

"A black ribbon on her hat, surely?" Uncle Charley protested in a mild voice. He gave Hattie what appeared to be a sympathetic wink.

As if it matters to me what I wear, Hattie thought,

biting her lips together. They tasted sweet, she noticed, surprised—probably from the one spoonful of sherbet she'd been able to swallow.

"Perhaps a *narrow* ribbon," Aunt Margaret agreed with reluctance. "We'll have to get her all new clothes."

And so that was how Hattie Knowlton's brief period of wearing mourning clothes ended early in May 1882—with a shopping expedition. She and her aunt bustled out of the Hubbards' brownstone the very next morning.

This proposed spree was due less to generosity, it occurred to Hattie, struggling to keep up with her surprisingly energetic relative, than to her aunt's discomfort over her appearance. It was as though the sight of her frayed hemline had hurt Aunt Margaret's pale blue eyes long enough. A poor relation was one thing, Hattie thought sourly, but a *shabby* relation must be an embarrassment to such an elegant lady. "I can't have you shaming us," her aunt told her as they climbed into the waiting carriage. "You must be made presentable."

There followed a long morning at a hatmaker's shop on Tenth Street, very near the Hubbards' home on leafy Fifth Avenue. "Not a child's bonnet, hear," Aunt Margaret instructed the saleswoman, settling into her gilded chair—exactly as if she were a hen planning to hatch a clutchful of eggs, Hattie thought.

"Certainly not, Madame," the saleswoman said, glancing at Hattie's chest.

Fourteen-year-old Hattie blushed and hunched her shoulders in an attempt to minimize her newly developing figure. She felt like a turtle retreating into its shell.

"Sit up straight, Harriet dear," Aunt Margaret said. "And nothing on too wide a frame," she continued, speaking to the saleswoman, who seemed hypnotized by Aunt Margaret's majestic manner. "Just a nice braided straw shape—tilting up, of course, to make her neck appear longer."

"Of course, Madame," the saleswoman said, as Hattie—now feeling even more like a turtle—craned her neck up as high as it would go in an attempt to fend off further personal remarks.

"Chin down, Harriet," Aunt Margaret told her.

"Or you might like the shepherdess effect," the saleswoman continued, speaking to Aunt Margaret as if Hattie were not present. The two women studied Hattie's reflection in the mirror, frowning slightly, and the saleswoman tilted this new hat to a more becoming angle. "The foliage is all imported," she added in a hushed tone, "and the roses are silk satin."

Hattie looked at her reflection, too; long chestnut-colored hair lay curled into an untidy roll against her slender neck. The corners of her mouth turned down. Wide brown eyes seemed to gaze imploringly at their mirrored twins, and the smudged shadows under them made her look haunted.

I look almost as frozen as one of Aunt Margaret's fancy dessert concoctions, Hattie thought. The comparison was a clever one and Hattie wished she had someone to share it with.

"Too much," Aunt Margaret pronounced, clearly referring to the style of the hat rather than its price—which she hadn't even inquired about yet.

"Something more youthful, with a rolled brim, I think," Aunt Margaret said.

"This style is neat and tasty," the saleswoman said, putting another hat on Hattie's head. She still sounded calm. By now, though, tiny beads of perspiration were spangling her brow. "Just a small cluster of violets on top," she added a little desperately.

Aunt Margaret stared at Hattie's reflection for a full minute in silence, and then nodded. "Very becoming," she said. "But can your modiste trim it with a narrow black velvet ribbon, do you think? The child is in mourning, and my husband seems to think it would be appropriate."

And so the sale was made.

Following a hurried chicken-salad lunch at a tea shop on nearby Washington Square, during which Hattie and Aunt Margaret barely said a word, the entire afternoon was spent at a small place that sold ladies' lingerie. This establishment was nondescript from the outside but as fragrant and luxurious inside as the hatmaker's shop had been. A plump, tightly swaddled saleswoman welcomed them as if they had happened by for a social call.

Hattie blushed as she removed her dress in the fitting room, ashamed to reveal her patched drawers and heavy woolen stockings, much darned. Aunt Margaret and the saleswoman exchanged significant glances. "We might start with some nice forms," the saleswoman suggested, averting her eyes from Hattie's painfully stretched ribbed cotton vest. "They're edged with Valenciennes lace. Thoroughly hygienic," she added, whispering to Aunt Margaret.

"Naturally," Aunt Margaret said, nodding sharply. "And she'll need some corsets, of course." Miserable, Hattie folded her arms across her chest.

"Our most popular model is sateen—very elegant. Seventy-five cents," the saleswoman added, whispering again.

Aunt Margaret looked at the woman coolly for a moment, as if disgusted that so base a thing as money had been mentioned.

Seventy-five cents, Hattie thought, much shocked. Why, that was near enough for a family as small as hers had been to live on for a day—or two, if they stretched.

Six snug corsets were duly ordered, and six drawers, too—three of soft muslin trimmed with tucks and flouncing and three of the finest lawn, adorned with embroidery, ribbon insertions, and Medici lace. A dozen pairs of hosiery were ordered as well, all black: three pairs of fleece-lined cotton, three pairs fashioned from Egyptian cotton, and six pairs made from a slippery wool cashmere Hattie adored the moment she touched it.

There could be three of me and I'd still not run out of undergarments, she told herself, amazed.

She'd never had so many clothes while living in Hammons Mill with Great-Aunt Lydia—and Joey.

The entire next day was spent at Aunt Margaret's personal dressmaker. Madame Honfleur herself measured Hattie with such care that it seemed to Hattie she must be planning to build an exact replica.

Madame was a slim tiny woman, her black hair swirled up into an arrangement so complex that Hattie thought it must have taken all three of her assistants to achieve its final splendor. She muttered French-sounding phrases to herself as she worked and hissed Hattie's various dimensions to her terrified assistant, who marked them down in a morocco-leather notebook with a trembling hand.

Even Aunt Margaret was awed by Madame Honfleur.

"A dress suit, of course—with two skirts, one for rainy days," Madame finally announced in heavily accented English. "Dark blue wool, with the skirts stitched around the flounce—twelve times!"

Aunt Margaret spoke tentatively, for once. "But she's only fourteen years old, Madame. Won't that look—"

"Twelve times," Madame Honfleur said, narrowing her dark eyes at Aunt Margaret. "You argue?"

"No, no, Madame. Stitched twelve times," Aunt Margaret agreed faintly.

"And the jacket is lined with black satin," Madame continued, staring across the room as if already seeing that elegant garment.

"All right," Aunt Margaret said meekly. "Black satin. Perfect."

Perfect, Hattie echoed silently—enjoying her aunt's submission to this imperious shopkeeper.

"Now, what about the wash suits?" Madame said, referring to the matched tops—*waists*—and skirts that comprised these everyday garments. "I have polka dots," she said, leaning forward with some urgency.

Polka dots! To her surprise, Hattie felt a small flutter of excitement in her chest. A stylish visitor to tiny Hammons Mill had once appeared at church wearing a sweeping skirt, its gored insets enlivened by polka dots. Hattie expressed her admiration of this article of clothing at their noonday meal, and Great-Aunt Lydia almost choked. "Spots are just fine— if you're a buffoon, perhaps, or a wild beast," she had finally said.

Joey had agreed with Hattie, though, going so far as to show up for supper wearing polka dots of his own—mud ones, all over his little round face! Even Great-Aunt Lydia had laughed.

"But, she is in mourning, Madame," Aunt Margaret said, clearly mustering all the courage she could. "Polka dots might be too—too merry, perhaps?"

Madame looked at Hattie with a new curiosity. "Ah,"

she said, almost to herself. "Mourning. This I did not know."

"But her uncle doesn't want her draped in black, not at all," Aunt Margaret continued, fibbing a little—not that Hattie blamed her, under the circumstances.

"I do not *drape* my ladies," Madame said, much offended. She tilted her head, and a stiff black curl popped loose from her coiffure. An assistant darted forward to secure it, but Madame brushed her away. "Linen crush for one suit," she announced, "both waist and skirt. Oxblood," she added, a gleam in her eye.

"Oxblood?" Aunt Margaret asked, startled.

"It's a color," one of the assistants murmured. "Dark red."

"I know that," Aunt Margaret snapped.

"Gray-and-white stripes for another suit—with a sailor collar," Madame said.

"*Oui*, Madame," the note-taking assistant whispered, scribbling.

"And for the third suit, I see a lighter blue—trimmed with white piqué stripes," Madame Honfleur concluded, clasping her hands and staring up at a point midway between Hattie's head and the ceiling as if the stylish outfit was suspended there for her to see. "A pure white waist— with a lovely high collar," she added.

Aunt Margaret cleared her throat and tried to intervene one more time. "But—but, Madame, her uncle thought that perhaps *two* wash suits would be—"

"There will be three of them," Madame Honfleur said firmly.

"Very well," Aunt Margaret said with a sigh, defeated.

Two weeks later, after numerous exhausting fittings at Madame's, Hattie's new clothes began arriving at the Hubbards' house. Although she tried hard not to, feeling it was unseemly to rejoice in *anything* under her own sad circumstances, Hattie loved each day's arrivals—the house slippers of the softest crimson leather imaginable, the shiny hand-turned dress boots, the petticoats, stiff tiered at the back, and a surprise from Uncle Charley—a down-soft dark green woolen cape for chilly evenings.

A billowing silk-embroidered nightgown replaced the flannel gown Hattie had brought with her from Hammons Mill, but she wouldn't let the maids discard the old one. She had it laundered one last time, kissed it when she was all alone, and slipped it under her pillow for safekeeping.

Little Joey had snuggled against this threadbare gown, hot with fever, coughs wracking his spider-thin frame. Hattie would not be parted from it.

Despite her guilty enjoyment of them, Hattie didn't really feel these fine new garments belonged to her. They hung embarrassed in Cousin Sophie's cedar-lined closet; it was as though they could somehow sense they'd been delivered to an impostor.

And what would Sophie say?

～ 2 ～

GLASS DOME

For years, Sophia Hubbard had loomed in Hattie's imagination as a paragon of all that a young girl ought to be. Sophie was good, Great-Aunt Lydia reminded Hattie far too often, and she was kind, and so well dressed, too.

As if anyone couldn't be well dressed if she had a rich father like Uncle Charley, Hattie always thought. Where was the virtue in that? And it must be easy to be good and kind—when you were full, warm, and beloved.

When Hattie moved to New York City after the last funeral, she finally had a chance to see Cousin Sophie and judge for herself what she was like. And, in fact, Sophie *had* been kind, genuinely happy to share her bedroom with Hattie. As the first New York City days passed, however, Hattie thought that Sophie was perhaps *too* kind and solicitous. Sophie watched her a little too sympathetically—

avidly, almost, as if judging each of her actions. It was as though Sophie was a shopkeeper who possessed an invisible scale that was able to measure grief itself, and Hattie was her first customer. Would poor bereaved Hattie cry if the word "brother" was carelessly entered into the conversation? Was she staring listlessly out the window a bit too long—or not long enough? Did she *pine* sufficiently?

Consider that first night, Hattie thought. "I'm sorry," Sophie had said, closing one of her beloved novels as Hattie returned from the washing room. "Would you like me to say a little prayer with you?"

"No, thank you. And you don't need to stop reading," she told Sophie. "I don't mind it if you read." She shrugged off her borrowed wrapper and tried to slip into bed before Sophie could see her shabby nightgown.

Sophie leaned forward; the gas lamp illuminated stray blond curls, transforming them into golden tendrils worthy of one of the romantic heroines in her novels. "But you must think me so—so flighty, reading for pleasure, after everything that's happened."

Hattie shook her head, mute. She didn't think that at all; in fact, she *envied* Sophie her ability to become lost within the pages of a novel. I wish I could do the same, she thought, sneaking a glance at the book. Great-Aunt Lydia hadn't approved of novel reading, however—not that there'd been the money for such luxuries—and so Hattie had never been able to form the habit of reading for pleasure.

"Let's *do* say a little prayer together," Sophie urged. "It will do you good." She started to climb out of bed.

"No—*please*," Hattie said, and she pulled the covers up to her chin to demonstrate that she was ready to sleep. Even with her eyes closed, however, she could feel Sophie looking at her pityingly, though she suspected the pity was more for Hattie's lack of dramatic flair than for her loss.

Hattie was relieved when Sophie returned to school.

The comfort of the routine and order of her uncle and aunt's household was seductive as March and April passed, especially compared to the sickroom chaos and clutter Hattie had lived with for months. And the Hubbards' house smelled a lot better than the cottage at Hammons Mill, too. Even with the occasional whiffs of horse manure that slipped over cool stone windowsills from the busy street outside, the fragrances of beeswax furniture polish, cut flowers, and freshly ironed linens were constant reassurances to Hattie.

You're safe, they seemed to say.

If only she'd been able to keep Joey half as safe.

Nothing was expected of Hattie during those long silent days. She breakfasted alone each morning at eight, sitting rigid in a gleaming side chair pulled up to the small table set into an alcove of the Hubbards' dining room. Aunt Margaret ate breakfast in her bedroom, and Uncle Charley prepared his own cooked oats in the kitchen at dawn as part of his health regimen, to the continued amazement—and secret pride—of the household staff.

The alcove's three windows were cunningly fitted out with tiers of scallop-edged wire shelves. Odd flowering plants nestled in little porcelain pots on the lower shelves. Snaky vines from unfamiliar growing things worked their way toward the floor from glossy plants on the higher shelves. With furtive looks at the long green tendrils, Hattie shrank against the back of her chair. She could imagine what Aunt Lydia might have said about such household greenery: "Sheer piffle! Might as well invite a pig into your parlor if you're going to start bringing the outdoors inside."

Hattie never knew what to expect for breakfast, neither was she asked what she would like. The menu was dictated from Aunt Margaret's boudoir. "Eggs, miss," the maid might murmur, whisking the top off a small silver serving plate, or "Fish, miss."

Hattie felt disloyal to her little brother's memory each time she tapped the bottom off a soft-boiled egg at breakfast. Why should she be the one to enjoy such fare—and every day, too, if Aunt Margaret so decreed? An egg had been a rare treat for Joey.

Aunt Margaret usually lunched away from home, as did Uncle Charley. Hattie was served on a tray in her room, ". . . to make things easier for the staff, Harriet," Aunt Margaret had announced after Sophie left. Aunt Margaret was thrifty in small, peculiar ways, Hattie had discovered. That probably explained why she'd been lodged in Sophie's bedroom in the first place. After all, there were bedrooms—Hattie didn't even *know* how many—that stood empty, in well-dusted splendor.

Seated at a small table near Sophie's bedroom window midday, Hattie nibbled at floppy triangles of thin, crust-trimmed chicken sandwich and plucked tasteless hothouse grapes from their stems, wondering where to hide them.

Alone in the bedroom during lunch, Hattie daydreamed, gazing around at Sophie's possessions: the long gilded mirror with the carved wooden birds on top, eternally frozen midfrolic; the dressing table swathed in the palest pink taffeta ruching imaginable—so pale it was almost white. How could Sophie bear to leave such a paradise? And yet she'd seemed happy to depart.

After her solitary luncheon, Hattie would look longingly at the room's two beds, wanting nothing more than to curl up on the one assigned to her and sleep every afternoon away. But each bed was dressed for daytime in a pink silk blanket cover trimmed with tea-colored lace and mono-grammed with satin thread. Hattie was afraid to touch such fragile fabric. The silk seemed to snag if you even looked at it too intently.

And so she dozed upright in a chair most afternoons. She felt like a porcelain figurine covered by a shiny glass dome.

Dinner was more of an ordeal. It was served each night at eight o'clock. At Great-Aunt Lydia's they'd eaten at six and were all in bed by eight. There wasn't money enough to keep the house warm enough to sit up late at night. At the Hubbards' house, Hattie's stomach was always rumbling by the time a small brass gong summoned the household to dinner.

Nightly, a beaming Uncle Charley helped himself to various chopped vegetables, which he clustered around a central mound of steaming rice, much to Aunt Margaret's barely concealed disgust. The food served to Aunt Margaret and Hattie was more elaborate: fish bathed in glistening creamy sauces and sprinkled with caper berries; tall crowned roasts still sputtering hot from the kitchen and surrounded by tiny browned potatoes, all pared to exactly the same size and shape, which secretly astonished Hattie. Often there were elaborate aspics; their shimmering perfection frightened her a little.

And there was dessert, always, unlike at Hammons Mill, where sweets had been rare, a birthday treat or part of a special holiday celebration. Here, though, there was a nightly parade of tall iced cakes, ice cream shapes encircled by soft ripe berries, or—terrible for Hattie, because of the shattering mess they created—cocky swirls of baked meringue sitting like little islands on jewel-colored puddles of fruit puree.

It was all delicious, but erect in her chair and feeling like a scarecrow that had unexpectedly been plunked down in a ballroom, Hattie cringed, awaiting each night's humiliation. Would it be not knowing how to use the serving utensils correctly? "Spoon under, fork over," she whispered to herself while Uncle Charley said grace.

She'd used only the spoon her first night, scooping roast vegetables from an oval plate like a baby. "A raw girl. I've got my work cut out for me," she overheard Aunt Margaret say later in a voice laden with self-pity.

Might she splatter the cloth with gravy or speckle it permanently with an innocent-looking berry? Or drop a fork onto the richly patterned carpet? Worst of all, Hattie thought, shuddering, would she again accidentally drop a buttery potato onto the elegant table cover, so blinding in its starched perfection? A tablecloth the visiting laundress had labored over for an hour at the long worktable in the big house's basement, aided by two housemaids frantically heating and reheating small black irons—or so Hattie had been told.

And then there were the nightly dinnertime questions. Hattie was expected to report on her day's accomplishments: her morning's reading—not stories, of course, which were prohibited before noon, but essays, history, the Bible, or other such improving fare assigned by Aunt Margaret—and the afternoon's supposed drawing or embroidery.

Somehow, the necessary words always made their way past Hattie's frozen lips.

"Tip-top," Uncle Charley responded to Hattie one night, nodding over the remnants of his chaste quartered apple and handful of walnut meats. He liked things to be tip-top. His wife nodded her head in apparent satisfaction, dabbing at pursed lips with her napkin, which she then placed on the table to indicate that dinner was finished. She stood up.

Each night Hattie stood up, too, relieved to have made it through another dinner. "Thank you," she said, hoping those words covered it all: their approval of how she'd spent her day, the dinner, their taking her—the poorest poor relation one could ever conjure up—into their magnificent home.

Privately, Hattie was expressing her gratitude that another long day was almost over.

Thank you.

❧ 3 ❧

FAMILIES

When the new green cape arrived, Aunt Margaret insisted that Hattie show it to her uncle as a way of thanking him. Hattie obliged, of course, turning for him in front of the sitting room fireplace like a jointed wooden doll. "Tip-top, my dear," he exclaimed, peering at her over his newspaper. He narrowed his blue eyes until the few freckles surrounding them disappeared, which signified that he was smiling.

Hattie turned one last time for his approval. The cape alone had cost almost four dollars—enough money to have lasted Aunt Lydia weeks. Well, one solid week, anyway.

Hattie scowled at the thought of how little they had scraped along on. She remembered the way dutiful Uncle Charley had visited them at Hammons Mill three or four times a year—as though he were performing a good deed by visiting a poor folks' home, Hattie thought.

Well, she corrected herself, that's what he *had* been visiting.

Uncle Charley always came alone. Sophie was away at school, of course, and Aunt Margaret hadn't liked leaving the city, Uncle Charley would murmur apologetically. Or Aunt Margaret was feeling poorly—or some other excuse. It fooled no one, not even Great-Aunt Lydia. And though it infuriated Hattie that Aunt Margaret clearly thought them beneath her notice, part of her was relieved, for it meant one less mouth to feed. In spite of Hattie's protestations, Great-Aunt Lydia insisted on serving their prosperous relative a lavish midday meal, no matter which of the few remaining pieces of Knowlton silver she'd had to sell to buy the provisions.

"But, Aunt," Hattie tried to argue the last time, "how is Uncle supposed to know that we're in need if you stuff him with oysters and Vienna bread?"

"*Oysters?*" Joey yelped, making a face. "I'll spit 'em out good, I will—right at the table, too!" His red hair seemed to bristle with alarm as he spoke.

"Calm down, Jotham. I'll fry you up a pannycake and smear it with molasses," Aunt Lydia soothed, more able to abide a display of insurrection from this five-year-old than from Hattie. "I don't want your uncle to know our troubles," Aunt said sharply, turning to Hattie as she sliced the fragrant loaf of bread as thinly as she could. "And, anyway," she added, "God will provide for us if we're ever *truly* in need."

"But, Aunt, God hasn't answered any of—"

"You simply don't understand families, Harriet," Aunt had interrupted . . . and she almost never interrupted anyone.

All right, she *didn't* understand families, Hattie admitted to herself, and so she'd been silenced. Her only recourse was to glare at her mystified uncle during dinner, particularly when he barely nibbled at the food. Bread and gravy, my fine sir, she'd thought, furious. That's what our supper will be tonight.

It was difficult to stay angry with Uncle Charley, however. He looked so much like the one photograph of Hattie's father, his cousin, that Hattie felt like flinging herself into his arms whenever she looked at him.

Not that she would dream of doing such an outlandish thing.

That one photographic image of Jotham Knowlton, Hattie's father, had been carefully captured just after he returned to Hammons Mill in 1865 from the War Between the States. Hattie knew it by heart from studying it so often. His long sandy-colored side-whiskers, curving elegantly down to his high white collar, framed a narrow, worried-looking face.

Perhaps the family should have waited before having that picture made, Hattie thought now. Maybe, given another year's absence from battle, her papa might have managed to hide the pain in his eyes.

Jotham Knowlton had been stationed in Washington at

Fort Stevens in 1864. That was when General Early made his bold attack upon the capital. President Lincoln even visited his defending soldiers during the battle. Why, her papa had stood very near him! Hattie knew the stories by heart: her father's dearest friend, shot straight through the chest and dropping like a stone; the farm boy—only fifteen, and crying for his mama—who Hattie's father had carried to safety. The boy's mangled arm hung limp as an old rope. "No more fighting for you," her father had said, calming the frightened young man.

Now, arrayed in her new finery and standing before her uncle and aunt in their overheated sitting room, Hattie pressed her hands together and silently repeated her father's dates as if they were charms that might comfort her: the battle in 1864, the safe return to Hammons Mill in 1865, the wedding in 1867, her own birth in 1868.

Then there had been the blank expanse of nine years until little Joey—Jotham, Jr.—was born. Years, Hattie dimly remembered, in which babies were longed for, expected, and—twice—buried following a brief struggle here on earth. Nonetheless, they were happy years, and they had loved one another's company.

Finally, there were whispers of another baby. Hattie had just celebrated her ninth birthday and was old enough to realize that something out of the ordinary was about to occur.

But within the week, her father had died of liver congestion. Hattie was bidden to kiss him good-bye. She was frightened by the way his frail body looked the same, yet different, when dead, its yellowy skin pulled down against the jutting bones of his face as if called home by the very earth that awaited him.

Ten days later Joey had been born, and a scant two days after that, Hattie's mother was dead. "Childbed fever," the doctor announced sadly. He patted Hattie with some awkwardness.

But no, the old ladies in church had said, shaking their heads, that poor Mrs. Knowlton had died of a broken heart.

Following Uncle Charley's hastily called family conference, Great-Aunt Lydia moved into the Knowltons' house to take care of Hattie and baby Joey. Aunt had been struggling in near poverty for some time, it seemed, and was in need of a place to live.

Hattie and Joey had been in need, too.

God brought them all together, folks said. He worked in mysterious ways.

Uncle Charley gave Aunt Margaret a worried glance, seeing the stricken expression that had crossed Hattie's face as she stood there in her extravagant new cape. *What's the matter now?* he seemed to ask his wife.

Aunt Margaret lifted an eyebrow, as if to reply, *How in the world should I know? I've done everything I can.*

Excused, Hattie fled upstairs.

4

GOD'S WILL

lone in Cousin Sophie's bedroom, Hattie straightened her back and tried to recite her evening prayer. "Our Father who art in heaven," she began, but it happened again: the image of her own father popped up behind her closed eyes like a fast-rising moon.

Her father, and not God, or even Jesus! Joey had once told her he thought God and Jesus were people, two *separate* people, and that they lived somewhere in the city, near Uncle Charley.

Now, *she* was here in the city—but where was God?

And what would Dominie Spencer have to say about her musings?

Hattie shifted to a sitting position and leaned back against the solid bed frame. *Dominie Spencer.* Such a silly, fancy, foreign-sounding title, *Dominie*, but one the fussy man insisted upon—probably to make himself more interesting, Hattie thought.

Suddenly, she could almost see Aunt Lydia's minister flip his pudgy white hand back, making a theatrical gesture toward a small plain casket whose meanness was only partially hidden by the drooping spruce boughs that had been heaped upon it.

So much illness since the war, the old folks said, so much dying . . .

Hattie tried quickly to think of something else.

Dominie Spencer was like a too-fat hunting dog, she mused scornfully. No, Hattie scolded herself—she ought never to blame a dog for the way he looked. If a dog was fat, it was because some human had fed him too much.

But Aunt's minister was worse than any dog. A dog would never turn his head and lift his chin *just so* as he preached, knowing that the sun would shine in through stained glass and illuminate his beaky profile for an admiring congregation.

A dog would never coax dinner invitations from people week after week and then expect, as a matter of course, to eat finer meals than his hosts could ever enjoy when alone.

And a dog would have more sense than to tell a person that every terrible thing that happened to her family was simply God's will.

God's will. Dominie Spencer uttered those words often— as if repeating them might make them true. As if saying the words absolved him from ever having to help anyone in need or give real comfort to the grieving and bereft.

Grieving and bereft . . . No matter how hard Hattie resisted, all thoughts led her back to memories of that last funeral.

Dominie Spencer had swayed slightly over the open grave. One good push, Hattie thought. She had stood just behind the Dominie. Moisture from grimy snow seeped through her boots, but her feet had been cold for so long that all she felt was a slight burning sensation. She embraced that discomfort; it was a distraction from what was happening. So were the wicked thoughts she was having about the minister.

At the funeral, branches of preserved bittersweet were tucked between the boughs—the very bittersweet that Hattie and Joey had collected for Aunt Lydia for Christmas. Aunt Lydia had put the branches into a stoneware jug and proudly placed it on the kitchen mantel.

"Over here, Sistoo!" Hattie could still hear her brother's high, excited voice. It seemed to echo among the gravestones, through time itself, and into Cousin Sophie's bedroom. She could almost see her brother's hair gleam against the tangle of gray winter branches swaying above the trees that lined Fifth Avenue.

The bittersweet's orange berries were faded by February, but they still provided some color, at least, a memory of joy.

Hattie had insisted on that.

The Hubbards' floral contribution—a spray of white gladioli—was perched uneasily at the head of the grave. Such expensive conservatory flowers looked as uncomfortable at the sparse gathering as Cousin Sophie and Uncle Charley did. The lush purple satin ribbons that held the flowers in place were stained black in places by melting snow.

". . . and usher Jotham Merritt Knowlton into eternal life," Dominie Spencer had brayed, lifting his face toward the cloudy heavens as if this were a favor that he alone could ask.

Hattie's heart seemed to contract within her chest as she watched her brother be buried next to Papa and Mama, near the frost-rusted flowers that still covered Aunt Lydia's grave. They had both died of influenza.

She didn't know how she could go on without her little brother.

Joey had always been like a willful monarch in their tiny household, and his adoring subjects, Hattie and Aunt Lydia, scurried to fulfill his every wish—allowing him to wear his floppy-collared shirts backward if he wanted to, for instance, or letting him fall asleep in the kitchen on chilly nights, curled up by the fireplace like a plump red-brown puppy in the worn old Sleepy Hollow armchair Hattie's mother had so cherished.

Hattie even crawled between his icy sheets sometimes, to warm them in advance, while her brother tried—usually successfully—to postpone his bedtime. "I'm waiting for something," he would tell them, pushing a wooden block across the bumps of the snug kitchen's one braided rug. "It's only for boys," he'd added once, embellishing.

In spoiling Joey, Hattie had realized even then, it was as though both she and Aunt Lydia were trying to apologize to the little boy for his orphaned state. But Joey had never known either parent. He was happy with Hattie—*Sistoo*, he'd called her, for "sister"—and Aunt.

But what, Hattie had wondered, was going to happen to *her*?

She had looked at the mourners. Her gaze settled on Mrs. Spencer, the minister's wife. A sweet, worn woman, she attended each ceremony at which Dominie Spencer offici- ated, with their seven sons. It was as though the minister needed a guarantee that he would have a good turnout for his every performance.

The Spencer boys were arranged according to size; their close-shorn heads looked like so many dust-furred stair steps, Hattie thought.

The littlest Spencer was picking his nose. A brother jabbed at him with an elbow when he saw Hattie looking in their direction. His elbow poked through the material.

The Spencer boys seemed always nearly to be bursting out of their clothes. That was something of a puzzle to Hattie; she'd have thought the law of averages would ensure that at least two of the seven boys would get to wear garments that fit. But no, on all of them ankles stretched past the bottoms of trousers, pale bony wrists shot past cuffs, and shirts strained against their buttons.

The Dominie was always perfectly attired, of course.

As if sensing Hattie's attention, Mrs. Spencer blushed and straightened the shoulders of her nearest son's jacket, nearly lifting him off the ground in the process. She then whisked a handkerchief from under her sleeve and handed it to the tiny nose-picker without even looking at him.

Hattie shifted her gaze.

". . . thy divine mercy," the Dominie said, and someone coughed, leading two or three others to cough as well, as if in mournful chorus.

Mercy. That was rich, Hattie thought.

She took a deep, shaky breath and looked at her Uncle Charley. He stood with fair-haired Sophie a bit apart from the rest of the little congregation. Aunt Margaret had stayed behind in Manhattan, of course, recovering from an unspecified ailment. She had written Hattie a letter of condolence, however, that was so refined, Hattie thought, it might have served as a model for how to write such a missive. Refined, and so cold.

Sophie delivered the letter, fabled Sophie—one of the three relatives Hattie now had left on this earth.

"I'm sorry," Sophie said, her dark blue eyes brimming with tears.

Hattie had packed up her few belongings; Uncle

Charley's driver collected them during the funeral, so there was no reason for Hattie to return to the little cottage. Sophie held her hand as the carriage pulled away from the churchyard and didn't let go until she'd led Hattie in the Hubbards' house, up the stairs, and into this very bedroom.

Hattie sighed, giving up on her prayers, and crept under the covers.

The memory of Joey's funeral, which Hattie always tried to suppress but never succeeded in doing, left her shivering.

5

HOURGLASS

Cousin Sophie returned home from school in June, arriving earlier in the day than had been expected. Uncle Charley was at his place of business, and Aunt Margaret was out having tea with a friend. A flustered maid fetched Hattie from her room.

"Cousin!" Sophie cried, hugging Hattie tight in the entrance hall. "Are you quite yourself, now?" she asked anxiously, holding her away at arm's length as though inspecting her for spots.

"I—I suppose I am," Hattie mumbled in return. Although it was almost summer, the hall's marble floor felt cold beneath her thin slippers. She gripped her toes to the floor as if afraid she might otherwise float away.

It felt strange to be welcoming Sophie into her own house, Hattie thought, but Sophie didn't seem to notice any awkwardness. "Mother wrote that we're to continue being roommates for the summer, Hattie," she said, pulling off her bonnet. A few blond curls escaped from her coiffure.

"I'm sorry," Hattie said meekly.

Sophie looked astonished at this remark. "Sorry? Why, I'm thrilled! It will make this place a little less lonely," she said, looking around the big hall as if it entombed her. "You might as well get used to me," she continued with a smile, "no matter *how* much luxurious privacy you're accustomed to."

"I suppose I must," Hattie said, trying to match Sophie's teasing manner. "It will be a struggle, though, and a sacrifice."

Sophie beamed a smile at her, and Hattie knew that, for once, she'd said exactly the right thing.

"It will be as though we're sisters," Sophie said.

"Sisters," Hattie echoed obediently. She tried to smile, but Joey's term of endearment rang in her ears: *Sistoo.*

I'll decide who I'm sister to, she thought, and was surprised at her reaction. For the first time since she'd arrived, she felt wide awake.

"Foof!" Sophie said two months later, strolling back into the bedroom. She fanned herself with a tear-spattered theater program and loosened her corset. *Yorick's Love*; Aunt Margaret had treated them to the popular tragic play that afternoon. Since it was inspired by a character mentioned—however briefly!—in William Shakespeare's *Hamlet*, it must be excellent, people had murmured.

Slender and self-assured, Sophie Hubbard was the picture of loveliness, even in disarray. Her eyes, huge and dark blue, were fringed with lashes so long that they seemed to sweep her cheeks when she cast her gaze downward. Masses of golden yellow hair—tumbling now over her shoulders—framed her heart-shaped face.

Hattie compared her own looks to her cousin's and found them wanting. She was taller than Sophie by at least two inches, and rounder in form. This fact embarrassed Hattie. Her eyes were as dark as Sophie's, but they still looked shadowed and haunted. Her nose was pert enough, but her cheeks—well, they were far too plump for true beauty, Hattie thought. And as for that silly round chin . . .

It was just as well she hadn't cried during the performance, Hattie thought wryly. Imagine her face blotchy and red with tears! Lucky Sophie's tears slipped out of her eyes like tiny dewdrops.

Hattie had felt like crying at the play for one panicky moment. But glances at the weeping ladies around her—some pressing gloved fingertips to the outside corners of their eyes as if such pressure might hold their hot tears back, while others crammed sodden handkerchiefs against their mouths to stifle their sobs—caused the tears in her own eyes to dry.

These were ladies who didn't have anything *real* to cry about, Hattie had thought furiously. For a moment, she hated all playwrights and other fiction writers. Tellers of lies, that's what they were.

Hattie plucked a loose hair from the smocked shoulder of her wrapper. She was too warm in it but was not comfortable revealing her bare flesh when Sophie was in the room.

Sophie—the veteran of three years' congenial communal life at Miss Bulkley's Seminary for Young Ladies—thought nothing of changing her clothes in front of another girl, of course. "It's so hot tonight that I can't think straight," she said, lolling back half undressed against her pillows.

"It won't always be August," Hattie replied absentmindedly. No, she thought—soon it was going to be September. Sophie would return to Miss Bulkley's Seminary. And what was Hattie supposed to do then? Hattie chewed her lower lip.

The whole summer had been like that, though, she mused. No one gave her any special thought. Sophie had rushed from activity to activity, trailing Hattie behind her like an awkward kite. Half the time Hattie didn't know what they were doing until they were doing it.

The girls walked for at least an hour each day with a maid trotting along as chaperon, Sophie always deciding which direction they would take. Sophie was mad for roller skating; Hattie—refusing skates of her own, being unable even to imagine mastering such a skill—held her cousin's bonnet, watching Sophie churn up and down whatever leafy, deserted side street they had found.

When it rained, Sophie played the piano while Hattie listened. If Sophie had a headache, Hattie read aloud to her.

It had all seemed so natural at first, Hattie thought— and Sophie's dominance was a relief, really, after the months Hattie had spent virtually alone. Even Sophie's chatter was soothing, like the sound of tiny birds clustered in a tree outside a bedroom window; Hattie was tired of listening to her own thoughts.

As the weeks passed, though, the rebellion that had sparked so infrequently in Hattie's life began to flicker. Why should Sophie *always* get her own way? And would it be forever so? What if Hattie felt like staying home all alone one afternoon, curled up and cozy with a novel of her own? What would happen then?

And the worst of it was—she would actually *miss* Sophie once school started again. How pathetic! Hattie flushed with anger.

Sophie had been studying her, a tiny wrinkle of concentration marring the smooth expanse of her forehead. "Even in a nightgown, you're more—more *womanly* than I, Hattie. It's not fair. Not when I'm a year older than you." Sophie tossed the program aside and looked ruefully down at her own flat chest.

Hattie glanced at her cousin and hid a smile. Sophie's loosened corset sagged against the bedclothes, and she had untied her bustle and swiveled it around to her stomach. Sophie's pale arms clutched the bustle to her stomach as if it were a baby animal that might try to get away at any moment.

"You're pretty," Hattie told her cousin truthfully.

"Oh, pretty," Sophie scoffed. "I'd rather be mysterious and beautiful. But there's plenty of time, God willing."

Plenty of time. Sophie *would* think that. Time must seem to unfurl like so many golden ribbons for girls like Sophie, Hattie thought. For her, though, time was something that was running out—like the sand in an hourglass. Those last clinging grains were the shining days that remained until Sophie returned to Miss Bulkley's. Sophie, her first real friend. After that, who knew? Maybe she'd be locked in the bedroom and let out only when Sophie returned home, as if she were an awkward, oversized doll.

In a sudden fit of self-pity, Hattie pictured herself caught inside the hourglass's empty cup, face pressed against the glass's inner surface, her expression frantic as it contemplated a bleak future: perpetual lady's companion, perhaps, or governess to other people's children.

That was probably what was being planned for her. She would be trapped, that's what.

And her loneliness would be worse even than her poverty.

"What's the matter?" Sophie asked softly. "Are you thinking about—about gloomy things again?"

She means Joey, Hattie thought, remembering with a flicker of bitterness the one time in early July she'd attempted to tell Sophie about her beloved little brother.

Sophie had interrupted her confidences. "God's will was done," she said piously. It was as if Hattie had crammed a hat on her head any-old-how or quenched her thirst by slurping water from a delicate finger bowl; an error in taste, rather than faith, had been committed. "You shouldn't be sad, you know," Sophie added. "Dwelling on the past is like—well, it's like questioning God, Hattie."

"Questioning God?"

Sophie nodded, solemn, and her curls bounced. "Mama says that God decided you should come live here with us, and we had to obey."

Hattie found herself nodding, too, as if she were Sophie's reflection in a mirror. She forced herself to stop.

"Mama says that wealthy people are wealthy because God wants them so," Sophie continued, "and the less fortunate are that way for the same reason. They shouldn't argue with God, and neither should we. 'The poor are always with us,'" she quoted piously.

"Oh," Hattie said. She smoothed her blanket. Well, she's right, I suppose, Hattie thought—I *am* always with them, aren't I? But her trembling hands betrayed her emotions.

"It's all part of His divine plan," Sophie said, smiling tenderly.

Hattie cleared her throat and looked down, pinching the

white linen of her sheet into the most even pleats she was capable of. She glanced up suddenly. "Is it part of God's plan for little children to catch the influenza and then die?" she asked. Her voice was calm in spite of the pounding in her chest.

Sophie nodded, solemn. Then, startled by the fierce expression on her cousin's face, she said, "It's not that He wants them to die, Hattie—but it *must* be part of His divine scheme."

"You're just as bad as Dominie Spencer, that's what!" Hattie blurted out, sitting upright in her bed.

"Domino *who*?" Sophie asked.

"Dominie Spencer," Hattie said. "He was my aunt's minister. Back home in Hammons Mill."

Sophie sniffed. "New York City is your home now, Hattie. But if this—this Dominie Spencer was a man of God, then I don't mind being compared to—"

"He was a man of his stomach," Hattie interrupted.

Sophie held up her hands, seeking peace. "I'm sorry, Hattie. I don't want to quarrel with you. I was only trying to make you feel better, that's all—by telling you how much we all feel you belong here. I don't want you to be sad."

Sophie looked so kindly that Hattie's first response—to ask her cousin how could she *not* be sad, given what she'd lost—seemed ungrateful.

"Thank you," she said instead. "I'm sorry."

"That's all right," Sophie said, instantly forgiving. She

leaned forward on one elbow. "Haven't you been happy, living here with us?"

Before Hattie could answer, Sophie continued. "The shopping, Hattie—don't you like your darling new bustle, and the evening gown with the dark green velvet bodice I persuaded Mama to have made for you? That nipped-in midsection, and those thirteen satin-covered buttons," she added reverently, as if the hand-wrapped buttons were pearls. "Not to mention the swag and rosette on the skirt. So stylish—it couldn't *be* more stylish."

"I like the gown," Hattie agreed reluctantly.

"And what about meeting all my neighbors on the Fourth of July, and hearing about my friends at school? Haven't we had fun?" Sophie almost pleaded.

Yes, Hattie wanted to cry aloud—but what about me? What is to become of me?

Instead she nodded, silent. She *had* enjoyed those things well enough—and the rides in Uncle Charley's new carriage, and the theater excursions. But along with the worry over her own future, the pleasure she had taken in these things was always muted by guilt, for hadn't Joey lain underground, swaddled in his shroud—the last damask tablecloth left in Aunt Lydia's linen press—at the very moment Hattie was being fitted in the bottle green velvet dress Sophie so admired?

In a strange way, Hattie felt *marked* somehow, by the sad things that had befallen her. It was as though the sorrow she'd endured from all those deaths had come together to form a ghostly bouquet she was obliged to carry with her wherever she went. Four black tulips, dusty and nodding, now: Papa, Mama, Great-Aunt Lydia, little Joey.

Her sorrow distinguished her, Hattie thought reluctantly—it made her different. It almost embarrassed her, she admitted to herself. Hadn't Sophie's neighbors, knowing something of Hattie's tragic past, nudged each other, gawked, and whispered when they'd met her?

And Sophie's friends were *Sophie's* friends. What were they to Hattie, other than rivals for Sophie's time and affection?

"Yes, I have had fun. Thank you very much," Hattie told her cousin, sounding as formal as if she was at an afternoon tea party and had just decided to take her leave.

Sophie jumped to her feet. Her corset fell away, revealing a loosely gathered frilly of the finest muslin, and her bustle bounced once on the carpeted floor, its ribbons sent sprawling. "Oh, you don't have to thank me," she said, exasperated. "I was only trying to say that you are *meant* to be here, Hattie. God wants you here, and so do I."

"Thank you," Hattie said again, with a little more sincerity this time. *She* didn't feel she belonged in this society, but she believed that Sophie thought she did. "We had a nice summer," she added, feeling that something more expected from her.

"And we'll have a nice autumn, too," Sophie said, pouncing gleefully on Hattie's bed.

Hattie shrank back against her pillows. "*You'll* have a nice autumn," she whispered. "You're going back to school—to be with your friends."

Sophie leaned forward, her cheeks flushed with excitement. "Oh, yes," she said, "but you're coming with me."

You're coming with me. The words echoed in Hattie's ears, and it was as though her heart were turning over, her emotions were so confused. Cool relief slipped over her like a silky chemise that had suddenly been dropped upon her shoulders.

Her immediate future was secure, at least. She wasn't to be locked up and forgotten after all.

But anger flickered, too. *Coming with me,* Sophie had said. Why, it sounded as though she thought of Hattie as a lap dog or a lucky charm—something to be packed into a trunk as an afterthought, almost!

And when had this been decided?

Sophie's brow wrinkled once more as the silence grew longer. "I thought you'd be so pleased," she pouted, looking as if a special little treat she'd planned for herself had been spoiled.

"Did you only now decide to take me with you?" Hattie asked.

Sophie shook her curls at such an idea. "Of course not, silly," she scoffed. She clasped one of Hattie's hands in her own. "But you're so cold!" she said, concern instantly transforming her features.

"I'm all right," Hattie said, withdrawing her hand and slipping it under the covers. "When did you decide?" she persisted.

"*I* didn't decide at all," Sophie said, a petulant frown changing her expression once more. "Mother worked it out with Miss Bulkley, of course."

"When?" Hattie repeated quietly.

"What difference does it make?" Sophie asked, flinging her arms in the air as she jumped to her feet again. "Isn't it splendid news?"

"I just want to know," Hattie said stubbornly. Had the decision been made a day or two ago, she wondered? Or was it weeks ago? Weeks during which Hattie had lain in bed far into the night, eyes open and heart pounding, worrying about her fate?

"I don't know," Sophie said with some irritation. She pulled a neatly folded nightgown from under her pillow and shook it hard. A virtual cloud of ivory lawn unfurled. Sophie inspected the gown with a scowl. "If that stupid maid scorched this, I'm telling Mother," she said grimly.

Hattie glared at her cousin for a moment. Really, Sophie was *impossible*. Impossibly spoiled, at least, and completely oblivious to what Hattie was feeling. But she was also generous—and clearly happy Hattie was going with her to school.

Hattie burst into helpless laughter. "You—you—you!" she gasped. Relieved, Sophie started laughing, too. She dropped the gown and climbed back on Hattie's bed. "Darling Hattie," she exclaimed, hugging her cousin. "You'll do brilliantly at Miss Bulkley's, I know. Mama tells me you're far more learned than I."

"I'm sure I'm not," Hattie protested. She *did* feel some confidence in her own abilities, however—why, poor Sophie couldn't figure coin change at all, and many of the fanciest words in her novels confused her.

"You were taught at home by Great-Aunt Lydia, weren't you?" Sophie asked. "Papa says she was something of a scholar in her day. That's probably why she never married," she concluded, matter-of-fact. "Do you forgive me for not telling you sooner, Hattie? I wanted it to be a surprise, you see."

"Well, I'm glad you didn't wait any longer," Hattie said, her voice muffled.

"But you're happy now, aren't you?" Sophie asked, settling back against Hattie's pillows. The two girls curled up facing each other—like gigantic first-course shrimps, Hattie thought suddenly. "There, you're smiling," Sophie said, satisfied.

Hattie reached out and touched a cool fingertip to her cousin's pretty little nose. How could Sophie, so generous and merry, and so privileged, with her cozy view of the Almighty as—well, as almost a business acquaintance of Uncle Charley's—be expected to understand the torments of someone less blessed?

Even if Sophie were forced to listen, there would be no way to make her understand the look on poor Papa's youthful photographed face or the sad curl of her mother's mouth. There was no way a coddled creature such as Sophie could understand how *brave* old Aunt Lydia had been every single day, clinging to the few remaining physical scraps of Knowlton prosperity while willing to sacrifice those artifacts for anything that would help the children—books for education, mostly, but also fine midday fare for a visiting uncle.

And there was no way to tell Sophie about funny little Joey, exasperating and spoiled at times—much like Sophie herself, now that Hattie thought about it!—but loving and loyal.

Also like Sophie.

"You're smiling," Sophie said again, contented. Hattie's smile was all Sophie wanted to see.

No, Hattie thought—Sophie could never understand these things that were as much a part of her as the very blood that coursed through her body.

Sophie was one of the lucky ones.

6

MISS BULKLEY'S SEMINARY
FOR YOUNG LADIES

*T*he Hudson River, gleaming green in the late-afternoon haze, disappeared as the hack drove up North Tarrytown's Main Street and turned right on Broadway. The ride seemed almost familiar to Hattie; at her insistence, Sophie had described it to her several times.

But Hattie was traveling alone today—much to her horror. Only the night before, Aunt Margaret had announced that Sophie was to accompany her to Rhode Island in the morning rather than journey up to Tarrytown with Hattie, as planned. Aunt Margaret's sister was ill again, and she did not desire to face this trial without family support . . . which she certainly couldn't count on from her husband, she added pointedly.

Uncle Charley selected a celery stalk from the relish tray and inspected it serenely. "Your dear sister is and always has been as healthy as an ox, and I have business to attend to," he said.

It was a very uncomfortable evening.

"Just like clockwork," Sophie complained privately to Hattie. "Every time I get ready to leave for school, Mother comes up with some emergency that she just can't cope with alone. And then she quarrels with poor Papa. It's not even that she wants me to stay with her," she added bitterly. "Mother just doesn't like me to have my own plans."

Well, that was all right, Hattie thought, looking out a window at the passing houses. She might as well face this ordeal alone. Sophie couldn't always be there to protect her.

When the carriage finally stopped, the burly old driver helped Hattie step down, and she handed him the hot twenty-five cents she had clasped in her gloved hand during the short ride from the Tarrytown Depot. She was wearing her oxblood linen crush, at least; the suit's stylish cut gave her *some* confidence, and Aunt Margaret assured her that the dark color made the outfit most suitable for traveling. "You look quite decent," she had said, almost surprised.

Hattie muffled a sigh as the driver hurled her brand-new Saratoga trunk to the ground in a surprising display of strength for one so aged. He dusted his hands together as if that were a job well done. "They expecting you?" he asked, jerking his head toward the big house.

Hattie swallowed and nodded. She tried to think about the building itself rather than the daunting people within who were—she both hoped and feared—awaiting her arrival.

Miss Bulkley's Seminary for Young Ladies sat big and square, its neat white-sided walls interrupted at regular intervals by windows—six of them on each level in the front of the house alone. The front door was where the fourth window from the right would have been, were it a window. The building looked as if a child had drawn it.

A tall narrow chimney anchored each of the house's four corners; it almost appeared that the massive dwelling—if flipped upside down—might perch upon those very chimneys. Or the house *could* perch on those chimneys if it weren't for the odd little two-windowed structure plunked right in the middle of the roof.

"That's the belvedere up top," the old man announced, seeing Hattie stare. "Old Mrs. Cobb used to perch way up there. She'd sit in her rocking chair, watching and waiting for the captain to come home," the driver croaked. He edged closer to Hattie. "Gave me the spooks," he confided.

Hattie stepped back as far as she could against the neat white pickets of the fence that encircled the property. "Oh, yes?" she inquired politely. Not a ghost story, please, she begged silently.

The last thing Hattie wanted was more ghosts.

The old man gave her a gap-toothed grin, folded his arms across his chest, and rolled back on his heels. "You could almost hear that rocking chair creak late at night," he said. "And her golden lamp would be the only light showing in the whole house. Made those windows look like eyes," he added, widening his own in imitation.

The two windows in the belvedere *did* look a bit like eyes, Hattie thought, startled. She hoped she wouldn't be assigned that room.

"My mama always called this the wedding-cake house," the driver continued conversationally. "She were fanciful, my mama were!" he added fondly. "I always thought the house looked like it was wearing a funny little hat, though. Lots of the old sea captains built houses like that. It were the fashion."

Before Hattie could think how to reply, a soft voice behind her said, "Miss?"

Hattie whirled around. Two maids stood just behind the latched gate, reddened hands clasped in front of them as if they were holding invisible welcoming bouquets. Their white lace-trimmed caps were anchored firmly to their heads, a good thing with the breeze that had suddenly arisen. One young woman had glossy black hair while the other boasted springing red curls yanked back into a bun at the nape of her neck. Each bobbed a curtsy.

I might be one of them—if it weren't for Uncle Charley, Hattie thought, startled.

"Hello, girlies," the driver said, leering his approval. The red-haired maid blushed, much to his apparent satisfaction. "Heave to," he added, aiming a nautical-sounding growl in the young woman's direction.

"That will be quite enough of *that*, Mr. Purdy," a woman's deep voice rang out. Hattie glanced behind the maids. A massive figure was gliding down the front walk. The woman paused at the gate, and the black-haired maid quickly opened it for her.

"Afternoon, Miss Bulkley," the driver said, not one bit cowed.

"Good afternoon, Mr. Purdy," the woman replied coolly. "I think you can safely depart, now—the girls will handle it from here. They're sturdy enough."

Mr. Purdy beamed a final leer in approval of this sturdiness. He climbed back into the hack, which lurched off down Broadway.

"The cheek of him!" the red-haired maid exclaimed excitedly, brushing at her apron.

"Simmer down, Gladys," the imposing woman said. She turned to Hattie and inspected her thoroughly. "Miss Knowlton?" she said at last. "I'm Miss Bulkley."

Hattie curtsied and ducked her head. "How do you do," she said, trying not to mumble. Miss Bulkley hated mumblers, Sophie had told her.

Miss Bulkley inclined her head slightly in response, then looked up and down the sidewalk as if there might be other members of Hattie's party lurking there. "Your aunt couldn't come, my dear?" she finally asked. Swathed in a shimmering gray fabric that matched her hair and rustled when she breathed, the headmistress could not hide her disappointment at seeing Hattie all alone.

Hattie looked down at her new shoes, unable to respond for a moment. Uncle Charley had remarked once that Miss Bulkley ran her small establishment as if the future of the civilized world depended upon it. Hattie couldn't help but feel that she was doomed to disappoint this large, impressive woman.

Miss Bulkley frowned, displeased with Hattie's lack of response, and her thick dark brows formed an almost perfect V over her nose. She smoothed a large hand across the front of her skirt. The movement reminded Hattie of the pendulum in the tall case clock in Uncle Charley's library. "Aunt Margaret's sister is ill again in Rhode Island," Hattie explained, the words coming to her in a rush. "Aunt Margaret wanted Sophie to accompany her, you see. But she should be able to return to school before too many days have passed." Please, God, she added in silent prayer.

"Too bad," Miss Bulkley said, and her hand swung across her belly once more. It occurred to Hattie that her new headmistress had dressed so carefully in the hopes of impressing Sophie's elegant mother.

"I'm sorry," Hattie said. At once Miss Bulkley shot her a look of disgust, and Hattie realized it was in the worst of taste to apologize for such a thing.

Two older girls—seventeen or eighteen years old, Hattie guessed—came clattering down the front walk just then.

Arms linked, they were dressed for a brisk Sunday afternoon walk, one in an impressive scarlet tam-o'-shanter and a matching fringed scarf draped stylishly over the shoulders of her dark blue cloak, and the other sporting a gray raglan coat with a black velvet collar. Their bright chatter made Miss Bulkley cast a look of disapproval in their direction. "Fishmongers' wives!" she hissed in a low warning tone, and the girls were quelled.

"Sorry, Miss Bulkley," the tam-o'-shanter girl said. She glared at Hattie a moment for being witness to their scolding, and then the two girls sidled out the gate and hurried away down the street. Hattie heard a scrap of laughter float back from one of them.

"Let's get you settled in, Miss Knowlton," Miss Bulkley said, ignoring this little insubordination. "Gladys! Fiona! Use the back stairs, girls. And mind the paint."

Hattie felt uncomfortable that the maids had to carry her bags, but she didn't dare to offer any help—she'd learned at least this much from Aunt Margaret. Instead, Hattie trotted up the walk behind Miss Bulkley and climbed the few stairs to the door without once looking back.

The school's front hall was big, square, and empty save for a large Persian carpet spread over the wood floor. A mahogany table—also square—sat plunk in the middle of the hall, and gas lamps illuminated the room, casting golden light upon its cranberry-colored walls. "All the way from China," Miss Bulkley said proudly.

Hattie nodded in what she hoped was a knowledgeable way, though not knowing whether the woman was referring to the carpet, the wall coverings, the gas lamps, or the table. She could smell meat roasting, and her stomach rumbled. "How very interesting," she said, to cover the noise.

"Ah, Miss Brownback! Miss Patton!" the headmistress exclaimed as two women descended the central staircase. One of them, short and round, appeared to be bouncing down the stairs, while the other, a tall, graceful woman, seemed to float. Both were dressed plainly in immaculate white pleated shirtwaists and dark skirts. The tall woman wore a gold engraved bar pin at her throat. "Two of your teachers, my dear," Miss Bulkley told Hattie. "Rhetoric, English essays, deportment, and drawing."

"I'm rhetoric," the round woman contributed. "Miss Patton, also known as Miss Pat," she said, introducing herself.

"How do you do," Hattie said, and she curtsied.

Miss Bulkley smiled graciously. "This is Miss Hubbard's cousin," she told the two women. "You'll be meeting her in a few days. Miss Harriet Knowlton," she added, inclining her head in Hattie's direction.

Hattie felt a pang of annoyance at this introduction. Was she always to be known as "Miss Hubbard's cousin"? This was not an auspicious beginning.

"We're pleased to make Miss Knowlton's acquaintance," Miss Patton said. She tilted her head prettily, so that the loops of her braids swayed like fancy curtain trim on a breezy day.

"My name is Miss Brownback," the tall woman told Hattie. "Miss Pat and I are new, too, so don't worry, you're not alone—although there *are* very few girls who've arrived as yet," she added, correcting herself.

Miss Patton nodded vigorously.

All of a sudden, Hattie felt exhaustion sweep through her, and she yawned. A little belatedly, she raised her hand to cover her mouth, but she wasn't quite quick enough; Miss Bulkley had seen the yawn. Her jowls almost quivered with indignation. "Flies, my dear," the headmistress said, and she patted at her own mouth daintily, demonstrating how this nicety should best be performed.

"I beg your pardon?" Hattie said faintly, but Miss Bulkley had already turned to climb the stairs. She beckoned for Hattie to follow her.

Miss Brownback bent quickly toward Hattie, trying to hide her smile. "She means to say that a person might swallow a fly if she doesn't cover her mouth when she yawns," she murmured.

"But—but I usually do cover my mouth when I yawn," Hattie said, feeling close to tears. *"Really."*

"Of course you do, my dear," Miss Patton said briskly. "Land sakes, anyone can see that you're a huckleberry above *that* persimmon."

Hattie was confused. Was everyone at this school so—

so *cryptic*? Miss Brownback burst into laughter. "Miss Pat is from Pittsburgh," she said. "And she likes to act as though it's way out yonder on the wild frontier."

Miss Patton sniffed and tossed her head, but she was smiling. "Well," she drawled, "Pittsburgh *is* to the west of here."

"I happen to have been to Pittsburgh, so you can't fool me," Miss Brownback replied. "Anyway, practically everything is west of Tarrytown." She started to laugh once more.

"Miss Knowlton!" an irritated if well-modulated voice called from the landing.

"I'm coming, Miss Bulkley," Hattie replied, and she smiled a quick, shy good-bye to the teachers. They were nice, she thought—and they seemed to like her!

7

"MY INTERMISSION: A RECORD OF SCHOOL LIFE"

lone at last in her room that night, Hattie perched upon her cot and smoothed down the first page in the journal Uncle Charley had given her that very morning. It was small—about six by nine inches, flat, and covered with fine paper decorated in a feathery pattern of russet, cream, and black inks. The book fit neatly on her lap. "Sophie tells me that all Miss Bulkley's girls keep them," Uncle Charley had said, giving her a mustache-tickly kiss good-bye. "They read them aloud to demonstrate their wit. Write something entertaining for us, Harriet dear. You can regale the table come Christmas."

Well! She had no intention of doing *that*, Hattie thought, but—as if she could feel the words—she ran her finger over the first two lines she'd written on the little book's first page: *"My Intermission: A Record of School Life. September 22, 1882."*

"My intermission," Hattie said aloud, as though she was making an announcement to the empty room. Her title, at least, must surely be original; none of the other girls would call their journals that.

The word had been racketing around in her head for weeks, ever since that tragic play they'd seen in August. "Is it over?" she remembered whispering to Sophie, when—just as the action on the stage was finally heating up—the heavy velvet curtain descended with a dusty *clunk*.

"No, silly—it's only the intermission," Sophie whispered back, giving Hattie's arm a kindly squeeze. "Perhaps Mama will treat us to a lemonade. Put on your thirsty face."

Intermission. At first, Hattie simply liked the sound of the word. Later, however, she searched out its meaning in Uncle Charley's big dictionary. The word was defined as being the interval between two periods of activity, she had learned, but it could also mean an interruption, or a suspension.

That was exactly how she felt, Hattie had realized. She was having an intermission at Miss Bulkley's. It was as if at school, she were suspended between her past life at Hammons Mill—and whatever fate had in store for her.

Fate.

"My intermission," Hattie said again. She looked around the room.

Clearly, it had been intended for Sophie alone. A much bigger bedstead—Sophie's—completely filled one corner, and a handsome desk took pride of place in front of the room's one window. A second, smaller desk of battered pine was crammed close to Hattie's cot, which had been wedged between the room's sole armoire and a dim corner. A cracked bureau—a poor imitation of the gleaming chest of drawers near Sophie's bed—kept the door from opening all the way into the room.

Hattie's trunk still sat in the middle of the room, although Fiona had helped Hattie stow most of its contents in the bureau before being called downstairs to help with dinner. "Please call me Fee, miss," she'd said. "It's short for Fiona."

"All right," Hattie said shyly. She knew better by now than to ask Fiona to first-name her in return.

Wavy vertical stripes climbed the room's white-papered walls in tints and shades of green, sky blue, and lemon yellow. The stripes were made up of vines and ribbons entwined; cheerful-looking birds lodged among them. Moss green velvet curtains had been drawn against the misty September night.

Hattie turned the page of her journal. Here, she decided to entertain herself with a rhyme. She thought and thought, and finally wrote:

> *In twenty years perhaps, I'll look*
> *These silly pages over*
> *And wonder that a decent book*
> *Should dare such trash to cover.*

That wasn't too bad, Hattie thought; if she were to read the lines to Sophie, her cousin would probably approve of those lighthearted, jaunty words. "Just be your own entertaining self" had been her parting advice to Hattie that morning. "Julie and Mollie will love you as I do."

Julie Wilcox and Mollie Brainerd were Sophie's two best school friends, Hattie knew from Sophie's summer stories. Hattie's stomach churned a little, thinking of meeting them—alone. "Jules and Mol will want you in our little group, I'm sure," Sophie had said with breathtaking assurance.

But would they?

Her own entertaining self. What did that mean? It meant not being morose . . . or tragic in any way. It meant telling no one about Hammons Mill or Aunt Lydia or Joey. Or about being poor. Sophie had said: "For all anyone knows, you're simply my orphaned cousin, Hattie. There's no reason to say more. No one likes for a person to hang out her misfortunes like laundry for all the world to see."

It was as though her cousin was ashamed that Hattie had nothing but her relatives' goodwill, Hattie thought. Did Sophie think being poor reflected badly upon *her* in some way?

Well, she could be entertaining, Hattie reassured herself. She *used* to be fun—at least Joey had thought so. And she knew how to keep Sophie amused.

Be silent. That must have been the gist of what Sophie

was trying to tell her, Hattie decided.

She had certainly been silent during dinner—not that there were many girls to talk to. Neither Julie nor Mollie had arrived yet, thank goodness, and Tam-o'-Shanter and Black Velvet Collar turned their noses up at Hattie when she said hello. She spent the entire meal sitting between Miss Patton and Miss Brownback, staring at her plate as if something fascinated her there as the teachers tried to engage her in lighthearted conversation.

And to think it was only a year ago, a little voice seemed to whisper in the lonely Tarrytown bedroom, *that you were snugged away in Hammons Mill with Aunt Lydia and Joey.*

Poor, shabby, and sometimes even a little hungry she'd been at times, especially after sharing her dinner portion with her brother, but at least she'd had a family of her own. A *real* family, Hattie thought, who loved her.

"Tragedy and poverty must show on my face," Hattie exclaimed aloud, and, stiff-legged, she walked over to Sophie's mahogany bureau. She tilted the oval free-standing looking glass and examined herself. "Why, I look like Papa in his photograph," she murmured, surprised.

It was as though she, too, had fought in a war—one that showed as clearly in her eyes as it had in her father's.

They'd both been marked by grief.

But—hair looked nice, anyway, Hattie thought, struggling to think of something else, something frivolous and fun. She patted at her forehead. At the very end of the summer, Sophie had coaxed Hattie into arranging her long brown hair into a Marion bandelette, the latest fashion. Softly waved across her brow, the rest of her hair was pulled sleekly back into a bun at the nape of her neck. "You're dark, so it suits you," Sophie had said, sighing.

As if having curly dandelion-puff fair hair were such a tragedy, Hattie thought, grinning a little.

There, that was better! She should try to smile more often, just as Aunt Margaret was so fond of saying. When she smiled, the shadows around her eyes seemed to lighten.

Returning to her small desk, she bent once more over her journal.

8

THE QUARTETTE

"Well," Mollie announced, as if settling an argument. "My mother told me that the Empress
Eugénie was a great beauty—a *raving* beauty.
No one had so small a foot or dainty a hand as she. And her
neck was long, like a swan's." She stretched her own slender
neck above the flannel of her nightgown when she spoke
these last words, as if hoping someone would make a similar comparison.

Hattie pressed her hands to her stomach. A nervous
flutter seemed to have taken up permanent residence there in
the week since Sophie had returned to Miss Bulkley's.
Fifteen-year-old Mollie and sixteen-year-old Julie—Sophie's
special friends—seemed almost unbearably sophisticated,
though they had accepted her graciously enough, Hattie
admitted to herself.

She worried, though, that she was not fitting in, not

truly, with the girls—this, in spite of Sophie's having dubbed the four of them "the Quartette" immediately upon her arrival.

All week Hattie had felt as if she lagged a step behind the others, a witness to, rather than a participant in, their daily merriment and secret late-night musings and confidences. She was quiet when they teased and bantered with each other. What if she were to say the wrong thing and shame herself—and Sophie, too?

So far, of the two girls she liked Julie best. The tall, cheerful girl seemed born to be outdoors, Hattie thought, demolishing her ladylike opponents in a fierce game of croquet or outstriding all others on their afternoon walks. Hattie wished she could somehow travel back in time to Hammons Mill with Julie—just a year!—and prowl the woods with her, kicking at skunk cabbage and searching for delicate woodland flowers.

She'd have introduced Julie to her little brother; Julie would have *adored* Joey.

Julie accepted Hattie without question. Mollie, on the other hand, seemed to study Hattie with a quizzical eye, as if trying to solve a particularly difficult puzzle. Not that she could solve such a puzzle, Hattie thought, sneaking a look at the flighty, fashion-obsessed girl. Mollie had professed an inability to open any of her three trunks without assistance, for example. Fee ended up unpacking *and* then ironing away the few creases from all of her clothes, which had been beautifully packed—with dark blue tissue paper protecting each garment!—in the first place.

Still, Mollie was kind enough to Hattie—even offering to lend her articles of apparel that might best complete an ensemble: lavender gloves, perhaps, or a black velvet ribbon to tie around her neck, or a red paisley shawl so finely woven that Mollie claimed it could slip through a wedding ring.

It was as though Mollie were trying to *complete* her in some obscure way, Hattie mused—quite without rancor, for in fact she did feel incomplete.

Julie grinned and adjusted the scalloped collar of her mapper, which is what all Miss Bulkley's girls called their dressing gowns. Her curlpapers jiggled. "How, exactly, did Queen Eugénie rave, Mol? Did foam pour from her rosebud mouth? And just how small *were* her feet? Could she stand up, or did people have to cart her around whenever she wanted to go someplace?" She slapped a sardine onto a hard round cracker and prepared to eat the entire thing in one bite.

Hattie had been surprised to learn that they were allowed to eat in their rooms—food that was sent from home in tightly packed wicker hampers—but Sophie said it had always been this way. Most happily, too, she added, since the girls felt famished much of the time, they were growing so fast. She theorized that Miss Bulkley saved money by allowing them to snack at will, though the headmistress prided herself on keeping a kitchen that was both generous and good.

The food was good, the girls conceded among themselves, though perhaps not as generous as Miss Bulkley liked to imagine.

"Eugénie was an *empress*," Mollie repeated, seeming awed even to be saying the word. "That's better than being a queen."

"I wish we had a beautiful queen," Sophie said with a sigh. She fluffed her hair absentmindedly.

Julie sniffed and settled back on Hattie's cot. The girls best loved gathering in this already crowded room for some reason, probably because Sophie was their unacknowledged leader. "You should study history, Soph—give it a try before you wish for a monarch, at least," Julie said. "And, anyway, it's easy to be beautiful in the history books," she continued through another mouthful of cracker crumbs. "All you need is for someone to write it down, whether it's true or not, and then people will believe those words forevermore."

Julie was the most scholarly among them, Hattie had quickly discovered, and the wittiest, and she had the sharpest tongue. As well as liking her, Hattie admired her the most. Mollie was the silliest of the group—but sweet natured, too, while Sophie was the prettiest of the Quartette, and had the most pride—which Sophie saw as a virtue rather than one of the seven deadly sins Dominie Spencer so deplored.

And what do they think of me? Hattie wondered. What is my role?

Sophie laughed, delighted. "That's what *we* should do, then," she exclaimed.

"What's that?" Mollie asked, confused.

"Each of us should fib in our journals about how beautiful the others are," Sophie said. "Then it will be an official part of history—we were all great beauties!"

Julie brushed crumbs from her mouth. "It's not as though we're so terrible to look at as all that, Soph," she objected drolly. "Not to require outright *lies.*"

It wouldn't require any sort of lie at all, Hattie thought, sneaking a look around the cozy room. Each of the three other girls sitting cross-legged on the beds *was* pretty in her own way. Julie was tall and lean; her coppery brown hair shone in the darkened room, even partly hidden as it was by the curlpapers, her pronounced cheekbones glowed with color, and her dark eyes seemed to flash.

Mollie was far more petite; she must be nearly as tiny as the fabled Empress Eugénie herself. Furthermore, her blue eyes were fringed with the longest eyelashes Hattie had ever seen on a human being, longer even than Sophie's.

And Sophie knew how beautiful she was.

As for herself, Hattie thought—well, Sophie had seemed to approve of the way she looked lately. And neither of the other girls was visibly shocked when introduced to her.

"I said 'fib' in our journals," Sophie reminded Julie. "We could exaggerate."

"Like how?" Mollie asked, fascinated.

Sophie nibbled neatly at the circumference of her cracker while she thought. "Well," she said, "for instance, I might simply mention—as if in passing—that my dear friend Mol has the tiniest waist in Westchester County. That she is *famed* for her tiny waist. That a grown man can clasp it within his hands, and his fingers will meet."

"Oh, write it, write it!" Mollie begged.

Julie rocked with laughter. "You'll be famed for something else if Soph writes that strange men are going around grabbing you by the waist, Mol," she finally managed to say.

Hattie cleared her throat. Was she really about to speak, to offer an unasked-for comment? She hardly dared believe it, and yet the room was warm, her stomach was full, and the other girls' buoyant good spirits were infectious. "And what if one of the maids were to come across your journal and show it to Miss Bulkley?" Hattie contributed shyly. "She doesn't allow us even to *say* 'waist.' "

Sophie smiled at her cousin, clearly approving of the wit of her comment and her boldness in entering into this spirited conversation. "Her *midsection*, then," she intoned, doing her best Miss Bulkley imitation. "And as for you," she said, turning to Julie, "I think I'll write that you have the longest, curliest head of hair in Tarrytown. Why, it's so long that you have to be careful not to trip over it! In fact," she continued, inspired by her own tall tale, "I think you *did* trip over your hair once. You sprained your ankle."

This was a good tease; Julie fretted over her straight hair. Her one vanity was to twist it up each night in papers, hoping for the tumbled curls that both Mollie and Sophie enjoyed so effortlessly.

Hattie settled back on her creaky desk chair. The flutter in her stomach was seeming to ease a bit, and she felt a shimmer of joy.

"And we all know that Jules has the tiniest ankles in Westchester County," Mollie was saying. "I've heard it said that Jules's ankles are so fragile that Mr. Barnum's gorilla could grasp one, and the tips of his gigantic fingers would meet."

Julie pounded the bedcovers, she was laughing so hard. "Oh, *that* will be a fine story for my grandchildren to read someday!"

Mollie yelped her glee, thrilled to have been quick enough for once to have made the joke.

"Shhh," Sophie warned them with a quick glance at the door. "We don't want a scolding from one of the teachers. Not this early in the school year."

"All right," Mollie whispered. "But now it's Hattie's turn. What will you say about Hattie?"

Oh no, Hattie thought, suddenly shy again. Don't talk about *me*, please.

"I know what I'd write about her," Julie volunteered

warmly. "I'd say that Hattie has the most tragical eyes in a three-county area. Why, if she were to go on the stage, people would pack in the aisles just so they could *boo-hoo-hoo* whenever she spoke her lines."

Theater had emerged as the latest craze for the girls at Miss Bulkley's, marred only slightly by the requirement that the students could attend only matinees—and they must be accompanied by a chaperon, of course. A Tarrytown play wasn't considered truly successful by the girls unless they had been wracked with sobs by the final curtain.

Hattie tried to smile, knowing that Julie meant her comment to be complimentary, and she reached blindly for the cup of hot chocolate that was on her desk. So people *did* see sadness marked upon her face!

But tragical was *good* in these girls' eyes, Hattie reminded herself. She replaced her cup carefully in its saucer and stared hard at the few oily sardines that were left on the plate. Her stomach fluttered once more, but she tried to match her expression to the jokey, easygoing looks on the other girls' faces.

"No," Sophie objected, as if sensing her cousin's discomfort. "Hattie's eyes aren't tragical at all—they're *soulful.*" She cast a glance upward as she spoke the words, as if demonstrating how a heavenly being might appear if plunked down in Tarrytown, New York.

"Oh, that reminds me," Julie said, after licking silvery flecks of sardine from her fingers with the delicacy of a large tawny cat. "There's a new minister come to town, Miss Pat says, to assist old Reverend Todd at Christ's Church. He comes complete with wife and an absolute litter of boys. And this is the best part, my dear Quartette—I'm told that we're to call him Dominie!"

It can't be, Hattie thought, stunned. The little village of Hammons Mill was a good hour's journey from Tarrytown, maybe more, and Dominie Spencer had wedged himself into his position there with all the tenacity of a winkle clinging to a rock.

But—*Dominie?*

Could there be more than one?

Sophie looked at her cousin curiously, recognizing the name. When she saw the expression on Hattie's face, she reached her hand out to touch her, to comfort her—but then she drew back, uncertain.

In an instant Hattie realized that her sad past was covered with only a thin icing of privacy. She had never spoken to any of the girls at school about her parents, or Great-Aunt Lydia, or Joey, either—nor mentioned the life they'd led, of course.

No, Hattie thought, the girls at Miss Bulkley's accepted her as Sophie's cousin, assuming that she, like themselves, had been raised in an atmosphere of privilege and luxury. And didn't Hattie have—thanks to Aunt Margaret and Uncle Charley—the wardrobe to make everyone believe that myth?

Hattie knew she could count on Sophie to keep her past private. Proud Sophie would hardly want her friends to know of a poor, raggedy branch of the family tree.

But count on the voluble Dominie to keep quiet? *Never.*

Hattie's icing was about to crack; shards would fall to the floor in front of everyone.

"I think the name 'Dominie' sounds nice," Mollie was saying. "It sounds *French*." France and all things French meant elegance to Mollie, even though Julie sometimes pointed out that there were bumpkins in France, too.

"Yes, but they're *French* bumpkins," Mollie would reply, steadfast in her loyalty.

"I suppose that's the idea—to sound French," Julie said dryly, "which means that he's probably an awful little climber."

"Oh, be fair, Jules," Sophie objected, "maybe he *is* French. Or at least a little bit French."

"Hattie looks as though she's just seen a ghost," Mollie observed suddenly, and Julie turned to stare at Hattie. Unseen by anyone but Hattie, Sophie held a cautioning finger to her lips.

Hattie cleared her throat again and tried to smile. "I—I don't believe in ghosts," she managed to say—quite firmly, she thought.

"Oh, *I* do," Mollie exclaimed, and to Hattie's relief, the Quartette was off on another topic.

*Soph came a week ago Monday and we four girls have had
a jolly time ever since. We have named ourselves "the Quartette."*

There, Hattie thought, closing the journal firmly later
that night—that ought to do it. She could create another
Hattie, happy, funny, and confident. And no matter what the
dreaded Spencers might have to say, that would be the Hattie
that lived on . . . at least in the confines of this little book.

9

GATHERED TOGETHER

Miss Bulkley's twenty-four students gathered together downstairs in the big double sitting room for prayers and Bible study first thing each school-day morning. They met promptly at eight o'clock, directly after breakfast, and stood in clusters between the room's two pianos.

The smell of toast and sausage still hung in the air most mornings, wafting in from the adjacent dining room, and light from several long windows filled the turquoise-papered room, filtering past swags of heavy bobble-fringe curtains and settling onto one of the room's three richly patterned carpets.

Black-and-white daguerreotype portraits of Union army officers dotted the walls like sober punctuation marks, black silken ivy garlands swagging the tops of their frames. These men were earlier students' papas lost in the war, Hattie guessed, or perhaps they were Miss Bulkley's own relatives.

Miss Bulkley led her girls in prayer each morning, but it was Reverend Todd who tottered over from the Christ's Church parsonage on John Street to coax the young ladies through the intricacies of the Old Testament, his reedy voice often trembling with either emotion or fatigue as he read aloud.

Gladys would answer the old man's surprisingly robust *rap-rap* on the door, take his hat and cloak, and lead him in to the girls, who were by then usually chastened by Miss Bulkley's spirited and often pointed entreaties to God. "Dear Lord, do Your best to forgive the silly girl who spilled the gravy on my best cloth last night," she might have been praying, her meaty hands clasped in pious entreaty.

The girls were always glad to see Reverend Todd. Now they could sit. They did this as gracefully as they could manage, the older girls claiming sofas and chairs while the younger ones sank to the floor.

Bible study ended at ten o'clock. Hattie felt confident up to this point in the day; religion had been an important part of Aunt Lydia's life, and Hattie was thoroughly schooled in the subject.

After Bible study, the girls' mornings were spent in the two-story addition that Miss Bulkley had had built for classrooms. In spite of Sophie's complimentary remarks about her scholarly abilities, Hattie spent her early days at Miss Bulkley's in a state of wretched nervousness. Would she be able to keep up with the others?

Miss Bulkley's girls studied rhetoric, French dialogue, English essays, mathematics, and deportment in the mornings, their classes staggered so that students of similar levels of ability were clustered together, regardless of age. Hattie had no experience at all in rhetoric, that esteemed art of using language effectively before an audience; after all, until seven or eight months ago her only audience had been Great-Aunt Lydia, Joey, and a couple of chickens. Neither was she particularly skilled in matters of deportment, or manners, although Aunt Lydia had done her best to instruct her.

Two days a week, then, fourteen-year-old Hattie's classmates were, shamingly, girls of ten, eleven, and twelve. Mondays, Hattie might struggle to declaim the parallel passages she'd so recently memorized: how both Nathan Hale and England's Joseph Addison had, for instance, regretted that man had but one life to give in service for his country.

Miss Patton wrung her hands and clamped her lips shut tight when Hattie spoke, as if afraid that otherwise she might interrupt the oration with well-phrased observations of her own.

Fridays, Hattie smiled encouragement to a pigtailed fellow student as they sat opposite each other, laboriously copying model letters from *The Lady's Guide to Perfect Gentility.* "*My dear friend,*" Hattie wrote in her prettiest copperplate script, under Miss Brownback's stern but sympathetic eye,

"I need scarcely tell you what you must have observed, that I always feel a pleasure in your society . . ."

But Tuesday, Wednesday, and Thursday mornings were for essays and mathematics, and on these days Hattie came into her own. She was quickly invited to study with the brightest students, which meant she was able to spend time with Julie. Hattie shone when it came to writing, thanks to Aunt Lydia's firm tutelage, and she was a stellar mathematics student.

Hattie even found that her fluency in French dialogue was passable, Aunt Lydia having drilled her frequently in both conjugation and pronunciation. "See? I told you you'd do brilliantly here—in spite of your youth," Sophie told Hattie teasingly after class late one morning. She smiled proudly, as though she herself might well take credit for her cousin's accomplishments. Hattie relaxed a little, hearing her cousin's generous words.

Afternoons at Miss Bulkley's were spent in the pursuit of the arts: piano study, both solo and duo, watercolor painting and drawing, dramatics, and chorus were activities deemed suitable for the girls to pursue. Hattie had never been near a piano, except when she'd turned the pages for Sophie during the summer, and she was reluctant to start lessons, as even the youngest piano student seemed to play brilliantly—at least to Hattie's ears.

She discovered that she had an aptitude for drawing, however, and so she was set to work copying an arrangement of fruit—carved from marble, so that the peaches, pears, apples, and grapes would never spoil. "They're always in season—and all at the same time, too," practical Miss Brownback pointed out, a smudge of charcoal marring her usually perfect complexion.

Afternoons were also the time for physical culture, which meant a brisk stroll around the garden, at the very least, or a group walk to the river. Bicycle riding was forbidden by Miss Bulkley, as she considered the big front-wheeled contraptions too dangerous for her girls, but croquet matches—when the weather was fine—were encouraged. It was rumored among the older girls that their headmistress might even place a wager on the outcome of a game upon occasion, but Hattie thought that most unlikely.

Julie was the school's acknowledged croquet champion, and Hattie tried to learn the game's finer points from her; how to whack an opponent's ball to kingdom come, for instance.

The girls read fiction in the afternoon when they could, usually retreating to their rooms to do so, thus avoiding the awful chance that Miss Bulkley might snatch an offending novel from a student's dreamy grasp and make it the subject of next morning's prayer.

Mollie was reading Constance Fenimore Woolson's *Anne*. She related its thrilling romantic story chapter by chapter to the Quartette late each night when the girls had stealthily gathered together. Miss Woolson's heroine was an orphan just like Hattie, and Hattie listened eagerly as Mollie read aloud in a halting voice, her finger trailing its way down each page.

Mollie's hesitant monotone made Hattie impatient; she could barely wait to read the work from start to finish herself, in private. She only hoped she would get the chance before Mollie sneaked the novel home to Bridgeport and back onto her mother's bookshelves.

Evenings, after dinner, the girls washed—"taking a birdbath," they called it when they used only a china washbasin. Full baths were taken twice a week, unless a girl was reluctant to step into the bathwater following her roommate, in which case she bathed once weekly. Sophie and Hattie chose to bathe twice a week. Sophie was always the first to step into the steaming water Gladys and Fee had carried up from the kitchen in heavy enamelware pitchers.

By the time Hattie lowered herself into it, the water had cooled considerably, but she didn't mind. Sophie was happy.

Most girls—even Sophie and Mollie—worked hard at Miss Bulkley's, at least at the subjects that interested them. At times, though, it seemed to Hattie that everyone came and went at random, arriving late to class or being called home from school because of family illness, for instance, or festivities. "Miss Brownback says it's a wonder we ever learn anything at all," Julie said just before lunch one day. Several girls were cleaning their hands at the downstairs washing room's limestone sink. Behind screens enlivened with glued magazine illustrations, invisible and inaudible by common unspoken agreement, two or three girls relieved themselves in raised chamber pots.

Minnie Bonesteel—Tam-o'-Shanter's real name, Hattie had learned—scrubbed hard at her inky fingertips, a scowl of concentration on her pale narrow face. "Well, I think we should only have to study what we'll need to know in this life," she declared. Minnie was even grouchier than usual, because Miss Pat had scolded her for inattention earlier that morning—and Minnie was a proud girl who took any correction as a personal affront. "We're not going to learn anything useful from a bunch of old maids," she added.

"Minnie!" Mollie almost squealed. Giggling nervously, she peered around in case anyone in authority was listening in, but no adults were present.

"Miss Brownback and Miss Pat aren't old," Sophie objected.

"They might as well be. They're never getting married," Minnie stated flatly, snapping the last few drops of water from her hands with a vicious flick before reaching for a striped linen towel.

"Not every lady gets married," Hattie said, her voice soft. "A lot of men died in the war, and—"

"I wasn't talking to *you*, you baby," Minnie said, turning to glare at Hattie, "and I'm tired of hearing about that stupid war. That was a long time ago."

"It wasn't so very long ago, and I'm not a baby," Hattie heard herself say. "I'm fourteen, only a little younger than you are."

"And not every woman is a lady, in case you haven't heard," Minnie continued, as though Hattie hadn't spoken. "Anyway, my poppy says that it's the stupid new idea of going to college that keeps a *lady* from getting a husband."

Mollie looked fascinated in spite of herself. "Do you mean because all the best men get picked early, while she's away at school?" she asked. Her tiny hands rested idle in the cool soapy water as she spoke.

"That's not it at all," Minnie said, a sneer in her voice. "It's that no worthwhile man wants a wife who would be such a poor homemaker."

"Well, then, why are you even at Miss Bulkley's?" Sophie asked, curious.

"Miss Bonesteel is here on her own course of study," Julie announced loftily to the growing number of girls gathered around the sink. "It includes gossiping, complaining, and name-calling. You know, the *useful* arts." She grabbed the towel from Minnie and started to dry her own hands.

Minnie put her hands on her hips. "I'm at this school under protest—and it isn't college. Also, my poor poppy is under the *illusion* that this is a school for nicely brought up young ladies from influential families," she practically hissed. "He thought I'd like being around others of my kind—not fresh girls and charity cases." At this last, Minnie darted a mean glance in Hattie's direction.

Charity cases.

"Don't you dare talk to my cousin that way," Sophie said, stepping forward just as Hattie shrank back.

"Oh, she needs you to protect her, does she?" Minnie asked sarcastically. "Well, I've heard that—"

A cool voice spoke. "You ought to try thinking before you speak, Miss Bonesteel," Miss Brownback said. She had just glided into the pantry.

Behind her, looking like a tugboat that had paused for a moment while pushing a more elegant ship out to sea, Miss Patton shook her round head and frowned. "You must think you're some pumpkins to say a mean thing like that," she told Minnie.

Minnie blanched, but then a look of false meekness settled over her face. "I'm so sorry. It was unkind of me. I'd better go," she said, sidling toward the swinging door. "You're right, *Miss* Brownback and *Miss* Pat," she added, shooting the other girls a small, sly, triumphant glance as she emphasized the word "Miss."

"Yes, you'd better," Sophie called out. "Others of your kind are probably waiting for you."

"Oh, give the school a little credit, Soph," Hattie said with unaccustomed boldness. "There *are* no others of her kind."

Her face blazed hot. Had she really spoken those words aloud?

Yes, she had; Minnie turned to look at her with cold, considering eyes.

Hattie shuddered to think she'd made such an enemy.

But at least she'd stood up for herself.

10

A VERY DELICATE
ANNOUNCEMENT

*C*harity case. *How did Minnie know?*

Dominie Spencer had taken the service last Sunday, as Reverend Todd was indisposed. When Hattie curtsied to him after the service, as was the unavoidable custom, Dominie Spencer winked at her as if they were fellow spies behind enemy lines. Sophie nearly fainted. "Don't encourage him—he might start babbling about your past," she whispered to Hattie, looking around nervously.

In the church's tiny rain-spattered courtyard, facing a leaf-strewn and somnolent Elizabeth Street, Hattie recalled, the Spencers' older sons had nudged each other with bony elbows as they goggled at her; even timid Mrs. Spencer scurried over to embrace her, voluminous skirts a-sway. "My dear!" the woman exclaimed, struggling between sympathy for Hattie's loss and relief at seeing a familiar face.

Sophie curtsied abruptly to the woman and pulled Hattie away before she could make an introduction.

Obviously, Hattie thought grimly, the Spencers had spoken about her, and word had somehow gotten back to Minnie.

She sneaked glances at her fellow students at supper that night, trying to determine which girls now knew what Minnie Bonesteel had said in the washing room.

Charity case. The words echoed again inside Hattie's head. Neither Julie nor Mollie had seemed surprised, she remembered. Did that mean they knew, too?

Sophie would never have told them, though, Hattie reassured herself. Sophie had made it quite clear any reference to her cousin's former impoverished state would be an embarrassment to her.

Lulu Callender was chattering away to Lydia Gilbert and Daisy Thompson at the far end of the crowded room's second long table. There was nothing unusual about that; as with the Quartette, Lulu, Lydia, and Daisy seemed to make up a self-sufficient unit. And none of those three girls seemed to be talking about *her*, Hattie observed with relief.

Across from Hattie, Carrie Henderson was shoveling spoonfuls of succotash into her mouth in a grim, businesslike way, as if fortifying herself for the long hours ahead. She and her roommate, Gertrude Spesh, battled nightly, loudly, and famously over whether or not to open their room's only window. Carrie liked fresh air at night, while Gertrude thought that night air was poison. Neither would budge from her position; the victor was always the girl who could stay awake the longest.

Some of the students laughed at Gertrude, but she never seemed to care what any of the girls at school thought. Her only concerns were for her distant mother; Gertrude spoke of her incessantly. It occurred to Hattie that if the school were to hold a specialized sort of examination, she would probably be able to answer more questions about Gertrude's mother than she could about her own.

There, *that* was amusing, thought Hattie. She squirreled it away to write down later in her journal.

Carrie and Gertrude did not seem at all interested in her, Hattie noted; they kept a wary eye on each other—the best they could, anyway, seated at separate tables. "Miss?" a shy voice murmured. It was Gladys, offering second helpings from a steaming tureen. Curly wisps of red hair encircled her face like a Renaissance halo.

"Thank you, Gladys," Hattie said, lifting the ladle.

Across the table from her, Minnie Bonesteel nudged Louise Phimley, Black Velvet Collar, and they held stiff hands to their mouths and tittered.

Hattie remembered too late the private correction Miss Bulkley—echoing Aunt Margaret—had already given her once. "Don't thank the maids," she'd said. "Especially not by name. They're only doing their jobs. *Nod* your thanks if you must, but look as though you're thinking about something else, my dear."

Minnie whispered something to Louise, who waggled her head in violent agreement.

Sharp-eyed Miss Bulkley, seated at the head of the table nearest the pantry door, lifted the little brass bell she kept by her water goblet and rang it once, hard. Conversation ceased, and every head turned in her direction. "Whispers are for secrets, and secrets are for fools," she announced to the table at large. Most of the girls looked understandably confused, since, unlike Hattie, they hadn't seen Minnie and Louise whispering, but Minnie Bonesteel flushed in anger and shot Hattie a look of pure hatred.

Hattie's breath caught in her throat like a fish bone.

"Now, listen, everyone," Miss Bulkley was saying. "I have an important and, indeed, a very delicate announcement to make . . ."

Sophie was finally asleep, and Hattie took up her pen to recount Miss Bulkley's surprising words, which had driven out her worries about Minnie Bonesteel.

> *There is a new girl coming, a naughty, bad, wicked wild girl. She is to be tamed and we, the Quartette, are to help or at least not to hinder in the training. No more naughty words are to be spoken, no more naughty deeds done . . .*
>
> *I am quite anxious to see her and only hope she won't bother the Quartette, but I think we will manage to have fun in spite of her.*

A new girl, Hattie thought, relieved, as she turned down the gas lamp on her desk and climbed sleepily into bed. Perhaps Minnie Bonesteel would turn her vicious attentions elsewhere.

Then she, Hattie, might enjoy another sort of intermission.

11

FANNIE MACINTOSH,
BY GOSH

She has come, she of the wild, ungovernable will and untamable nature. Our wildest conjectures have failed and she exceeds all that we feared or dared to imagine. Miss Brownback has a headache. Sophie has a headache. Mollie has a headache.

Her name is Fannie Macintosh, by gosh, and of all mixtures, contradictions, whirlwinds, tornadoes, earthquakes, etc., she goes ahead, she is a compound of all.

Language fails when you wish to describe her . . .

Hattie sat back and nibbled at the end of her pen. Writing in her journal was fun, she decided; she'd never had an experience quite like it. In Hammons Mill, there hadn't been time to *have* a thought, much less examine it. And at Miss Bulkley's, it was the quickest girls whose words were heard.

Even when the Quartette got together for a cozy chat, it was rarely Hattie who spoke first. Sophie took center stage when the topic turned to the intricacies of the society around them, Mollie had final say in matters of fashion, and Julie offered the wittiest observations on just about any subject. That subject changed frequently, too, and lightning fast.

Hattie merely chimed in.

In her journal, however, she found that for the first time in her life she was able to explore a thought, following it to its natural conclusion—without fear of contradiction or interruption. Hattie had never had this luxury before.

Her journal was the only thing that was truly hers.

She adjusted the sputtering light of her lamp and looked over at the huddled form on Sophie's bed. "Can I get you something to eat?" she asked her cousin. "Would that make you feel better?"

"*Uhhh*," Sophie said, clasping a damp washcloth to her forehead. Her fingertips were wrinkled from the wet, and the golden hair around her face seemed to have sprung into a new curly life of its own under the moistened cloth.

"I can sneak downstairs and see if I can find you a handful of gingersnaps or some cup custard," Hattie suggested, sympathetic. "Fee said she'd hide something for you in the kitchen in case you got hungry later." Sophie had felt so queasy from her headache that she'd been unable to eat her dinner.

"*Uhhh*," Sophie said again, but she peeked out from

under the washcloth this time. She actually *was* beginning to look a little hungry, Hattie was relieved to see.

"I'll go," Hattie said, springing to her feet.

"No, stop," Sophie said, sitting up. The washcloth dropped to her lap. "What if *she* sees you?"

She. Sophie didn't even need to utter the name, Hattie thought. Why, Minnie Bonesteel, their old nemesis, had paled instantly in comparison to Fannie Macintosh, by gosh. Not that Hattie found Fannie frightening in any way. No, Fannie was vivid—and appealing. A person had no idea what she would say or do next! "What if she does see me?" she asked Sophie, pausing.

"Oh, Hattie, she may figure that there's something she neglected to tell us today. Seeing you might give her the idea to come into our room for another 'little chat.' " Sophie uttered those last words in a voice filled with dread.

Hattie sat down on the edge of Sophie's bed. She picked up the limp warm washcloth and twirled it in the air to cool it in case her cousin needed it again. "Fannie did tell us a tiny bit about herself today, didn't she," she teased.

"A *tiny* bit?" Sophie asked, her blue eyes wide with incredulity.

"And I suppose it may also be said that she's not blind to her own charms," Hattie continued, watching the cloth go around and around.

"Blind to them?" Sophie practically squawked. "She trumpets them!"

Hattie giggled. It was too tempting to resist, she thought; her droll, journal-inspired words had diverted Sophie. This was power!

She held up her hand as if to say *Wait*, and then rushed over to her little desk. "Listen to this—I want you to hear something," she said, picking up her journal. For the first time, she read her words out loud.

> *She has read poetry to us, recited, sung, talked <u>a little</u> of herself, just so we should not forget her, changed all our names, admired all our family pictures, especially those of our brothers, expressed her opinion, not favorable! about the town, school, and its inhabitants, declared that if there are eight thousand in the place, which fact she doubts, they must all be women and children, and has expressed her intention to go to the church which can boast the most fellows . . .*
>
> *And she came yesterday at ten o'clock.*

Sophie was giggling by now, her headache forgotten. "Oh, Hattie," she said, "when did you *write* that?"

"Just now," Hattie said, thrilled at her cousin's response. "While you were busy groaning."

"You have to read it to the others this very minute," Sophie announced, springing to her feet, headache gone. "They'll hear for themselves what a wit you can be! And it will give us all strength."

"No, wait," Hattie cried, and Sophie paused halfway to the door. "It's late, Soph—it's after nine. We're supposed to be asleep." She didn't mind reading *Sophie* parts of her journal, but . . .

"Oh, please," Sophie begged. "Let me read it, if you don't want to. It—it will help your reputation."

My reputation.

This, Hattie knew, was the closest Sophie would come to referring to what Minnie Bonesteel said in the washing room.

"Besides, Hattie, you were about to creep downstairs to the kitchen to hunt me up something to eat, weren't you?" Sophie continued.

Hattie was still worried. "But—but listen, Soph, I'm just not certain that I want anyone to read my journal," she finally said. Her written words—or the act of writing them—was something that had become precious to her, she realized. Giving in to temptation and sharing her private thoughts with Sophie was one thing, but—trotting them out to entertain the Quartette?

And anyway, she thought, she'd deliberately exaggerated the day's events just to be funny. To amuse *herself*.

Sophie looked puzzled. She sat back down on the edge of her bed and pulled on her house slippers. "But you just read it to me, and that's what they're for," she said. "I mean," she added, "it's why we *write* them."

"We haven't read them to each other yet," Hattie objected stubbornly.

"That's because no one's had anything interesting to say

up until now. But Miss Macintosh has fixed *that*," Sophie stated.

Hattie clasped her journal to her chest and bit her lower lip. "But I—I *like* Fannie Macintosh," she finally surprised herself by saying. "At least a little bit."

She wondered at her own words. Did she truly like Fannie, or was she simply feeling sorry for her? Although a more unlikely person for whom to feel sorry was difficult to imagine. Why, Fannie Macintosh could whip her weight in wildcats, as Miss Pat would say.

Sophie frowned. Her pale yellow curls tumbled around her face, which was flushed pink with incredulity. "You *like* her?" she asked. "But, Hattie, she's—she's—she says '*I reckon!*' And at supper, she asked for a chicken breast! *Breast*, Hattie. She didn't even have the delicacy to say 'bosom.'"

"I know," Hattie conceded. "But her father is practically a cowboy, Sophie. Maybe she doesn't know any better." Hattie thought of her own many social transgressions since she'd left Hammons Mill. She'd complimented Aunt Margaret on her pretty gown once, only to be reproved, "No personal comments, please, Harriet—negative *or* positive."

Another time, she'd overheard Uncle Charley laughingly, if lovingly, mimic her to his wife, saying, "I liked all the little *fixins* we had at dinner."

Even Sophie had to explain after tea one day why you should never ask if a person would like *more* of something, because it implied a kind of piggishness. "You simply inquire if they'd like some cake, even if it's their fourth slice and they have cake coming out of their ears," Sophie had explained earnestly.

"Fannie's father is not a cowboy, Hattie, even if he really did witness that awful shootout last year, which statement I sincerely doubt," Sophie objected now, her blue eyes troubled. "And her clothes! Did you see the size of the bustle she wore today?"

Hattie smoothed her cousin's soft blue blanket. She had liked Fannie's canary yellow ensemble; it was a change, anyway, from the snowy white shirtwaists and dark skirts most girls wore to class.

And it's only because of Aunt Margaret's pride that *I* have new clothes—in styles most refined, and of the highest quality, Hattie thought, silently mimicking her aunt.

"We all wear bustles here," she murmured, "except for the very youngest girls."

"Yes, but we wear cunning *little* ones," Sophie replied smugly. "Fannie looked as if she was about to fall over backwards. And her petticoat! Taffeta, in broad daylight, and red-and-purple stripes. *My dear!*" she concluded, Aunt Margaret-style.

Hattie sighed. She didn't like hearing Sophie take against someone so quickly. It was a bit alarming, really. Why, what if Sophie had taken against *her*, in a similar way?

Or what if she decided to do so at some future date?

"Anyway," Sophie continued, lifting her chin in the air,

"Fannie has a mother, hasn't she? Her mother should certainly have taught her to mind her Ps and Qs. If she isn't some dance-hall hostess in Tombstone, Arizona, I mean."

But Fannie didn't have a mother. She and Hattie had found themselves alone in the washing room, and she'd told Hattie so, quietly, having heard that she was an orphan. "My ma's in heaven, too," she whispered, staring down at her shiny black boots. "Don't tell the others, though."

Don't tell the others. Hattie understood that feeling completely.

She hadn't known what to say, so she simply squeezed the new girl's hand in sympathy.

"Maybe—maybe Fannie's mother is dead," Hattie said to Sophie. Making such a suggestion wasn't betraying a confidence, she reassured herself.

"Oh, phooey!" Sophie exclaimed, pounding the bed with her fist. "That can't be *everyone's* excuse for bad manners."

Hattie rose to her feet blindly, stunned by her cousin's cruel words. Her journal fell to the floor unnoticed. Was Sophie saying that *she* had bad manners? Or that she was using her family's tragedy as a sort of—an *apology* for her own ignorance or social clumsiness?

Sophie was on her feet, too. "Hattie, darling, I didn't mean it," she said, instantly contrite. She took one of Hattie's cold hands between her two warm ones and pressed it tenderly. "I was only trying to say that I'll bet *Fannie* will try to use her mother's absence as an excuse—if that's even true, which I don't think it is."

"Oh," Hattie said. Her face felt stiff, as if she'd been standing outside in a cold wind for hours.

"Listen," Sophie said in her most winning way, as she tugged her cousin back to the bed. "Sit," she instructed, and Hattie perched uneasily on the edge of Sophie's bed, waiting to hear what Sophie had to say. Her expression was solemn; Sophie looked like a silly little owl, Hattie thought suddenly.

"It's like this," Sophie said. "You simply *can't* be friends with girls like Mollie and Julie and me if you're friends with someone like Fannie Macintosh, too. Don't you want to be part of the Quartette, Hattie?"

Hattie nodded, mute, but her heart seemed to skip a beat. This sounded like a threat! How could Sophie—who claimed to love her—say such a thing?

"Now," Sophie said, as though she were reasoning out some rhetorical puzzle Miss Pat had posed, "my mother would say that girls like Fannie Macintosh are sent to test us, Hattie. If we fall into their ways, it means that we're one sort of person, while if we uphold our standards it means we're the other sort of person."

And Sophie thinks that I might as easily go in one direction as the other, Hattie thought, blushing. "But—but we don't *know* Fannie's ways," she objected weakly. "Not yet."

Sophie folded her arms across her chest—appearing

alarmingly like Aunt Margaret for a moment, Hattie thought. "I know everything there is to know about Fannie simply by looking at her," Sophie announced. "The only thing I *don't* know is how she even came to be admitted to Miss Bulkley's in the first place! We're supposed to be exclusive here—which ought to mean that girls like Fannie are kept out."

Hattie swallowed, startled by her cousin's vehemence. It was as though the little embers from the glowing coals of Aunt Margaret's snobbery, which Hattie knew always smoldered in Sophie, had suddenly burst into flame.

"Minnie says it must simply be a matter of money," Sophie continued. "A heap of gold nuggets must have been paid for the privilege of attending our school. Minnie says that she, for one, plans to inform her poppy about it, and Gertrude has already written to her mama."

"Maybe Minnie's poppy will come and take her away," Hattie said, faint hope glimmering.

"Or perhaps someone will come and take *Fannie Macintosh* away," Sophie said with a scowl. Then she yawned, stretched, and smiled with all of her old charm. "Why, I think I've been quite cured of Macintosh fever."

"I'm glad of that, anyway," Hattie said. Her feeble defense of Fannie echoed in her now-aching head, though, as did Sophie's denouncement of Fannie—and her implied threat to Hattie.

Sophie leaned forward, her cheeks flushed. "I know—

let's *both* sneak downstairs for some gingersnaps, why don't we?"

"I—I suppose we could go look for some cookies," Hattie said slowly.

"And I suppose we should!" Sophie exclaimed. "We're both cousins and best friends, after all. We must stick together, Hattie."

"I suppose so," Hattie said in a joking tone of voice.

Her troubled eyes, however, betrayed her true feelings.

12

MACINTOSH VERSUS
BONESTEEL

*T*he mice discovered one of my dresses, and ate part of both sleeves. Were there cookies on the floor? Oh! No, indeed! There was only <u>a</u> cookie, one little innocent gingersnap, and the waist of a dress. Now the cookie is gone, and some chewed-up woolen stuff adorns a mouse hole. I nearly said a rat hole but remembered just in time what Miss Bulkley said to me when I said there were <u>rats</u> in our room.

"<u>Hattie</u>! What! <u>Rats</u>! <u>Never-r-r</u> say that word again, we have never had <u>rats</u> in this house! There may be mice, but even mice would not come unless there was something to come for. But as for <u>rats</u>, <u>never-r-r</u>."

And I said, excuse me, I thought rats and mice were the same thing. Of course, I knew rats were the males and mice the females. (I thought she was mad because I hinted there were <u>males</u> in the house.)

She was not silenced, but said in tones of contempt, "Hattie Knowlton, <u>don't</u> you know better than that? They are <u>entirely</u> different."

Then she explained, and I retired.

Writing about this incident was making Hattie smile for the first time in days. Miss Bulkley became so—so *jangled* whenever any of her girls mentioned the differences between ladies and gentlemen! "Soon enough," she'd say darkly.

Sophie burst into the room. "Come with me," she whispered, much excited. "You're missing the whole thing." She tugged at her cousin's nightgown sleeve. "Come on, Hattie—before Miss Pat or Miss Brownback finds out we're all awake."

Hattie climbed out of bed and grabbed her quilt to wrap around her. She stumbled on a streak of moonlight that seemed to puddle on the carpet, fading its tangled pattern. "Ow," she complained as Sophie pulled her along.

"Come *on*," Sophie urged again. "It's Macintosh versus Bonesteel, and they are really going at it. My dear," she added archly, "you should hear the language!"

"I thought we didn't like Minnie," Hattie said, "after—you know, after what she said that day." *Charity case.* But Sophie's hand was already on the doorknob. "You told the Quartette only yesterday that she looked as though she'd been weaned on a sour pickle."

"We don't like either one of them," Sophie whispered

instructively as they stepped into the icy hall, "but that doesn't mean we have to miss all the fun."

"Fun," Hattie grumbled, shivering. Obedient, though, she trotted after her cousin. Sophie's pale hair seemed to shimmer in the gloom of the hall; skeletal branches blown about by the cold November wind ticked and clacked against a long window's uncurtained panes.

Sophie rapped twice at Minnie's bedroom door, and it opened only wide enough for a long-lashed eye to peer out at them. The eye blinked once. "Oh, for heaven's sake—it's only us, Mol," Sophie said impatiently, and she pushed her way inside, dragging Hattie behind her.

It was the first time Hattie had been in Minnie's room, which was one of the school's few unshared bedrooms. The room's yellow-speckled wallpaper, mustard curtains, and ivory-painted trim seemed to cast an eerie glow over the girls assembled there.

Hattie blinked at the tableau that greeted her: Minnie Bonesteel, Louise Phimley, and Gertrude Spesh were perched on Minnie's rumpled bed. They were illuminated by the gas lamp that flickered atop Minnie's bedside table, each girl wrapped in a quilt or blanket against the room's chill. Gertrude, in particular, was an almost unrecognizable lump of blanket, save for a small circle of face.

Across the room, huddled near the fireplace, sat Carrie Henderson, Lulu Callender, and Julie Wilcox. Having admitted Sophie and Hattie, Mollie rejoined them; Julie held out the corner of a quilt for her, wrapping her into its coziness as she sank to her heels.

Alone, silhouetted in the watery moonlight that streamed through the window, stood Fannie Macintosh, arms folded. She was glaring at Minnie; her eyes never flicked once toward Hattie. The girls had not, in fact, exchanged any words since Fannie's first full day at school. Hattie hadn't dared—not after Sophie's threat.

Fannie looked magnificent, Hattie thought. The jade-green silk of her nightgown fell from a pointed yoke and swirled around her ankles, and her bare feet seemed rooted to the floor. Unbound, her black hair cascaded in lavish curls well past her shoulders. Her cheeks burned pink, standing out against the whiteness of her face.

With neither quilt nor blanket to warm her she must have been freezing, but Fannie seemed not to notice the cold; perhaps rage was lending her warmth.

Sophie took Hattie's hand and led her to the little group near the fire.

"It's *true*," Minnie said, resuming the dialogue that Sophie and Hattie had interrupted. "It probably happens all the time."

"Liar," Fannie said, white-faced.

"I'm not lying," Minnie said, her voice calm. "I read about it in a magazine, didn't I?" Louise nodded, as if she had been a witness to that very event. "Why," Minnie continued, barely concealing a malicious smile, "haven't you heard of the Society for the Prevention of People Being Buried Alive?"

Buried alive. Hattie felt a shiver creep down her back. She tried not to think of little Joey in his coffin.

"*I've* heard about that society, and so has Mama," Gertrude said from her cocoon of blankets, scarves, and quilts. "I thought everyone had."

Hattie hadn't.

"My mother was not buried alive, you polecat," Fannie said through gritted teeth. She looked at Hattie for a second; the expression in her eyes made Hattie catch her breath.

I didn't tell! she wanted to shout, but no words came. She shook her head slightly, but Fannie looked away, hurt.

Minnie shook her head pityingly. "I'm afraid you really have no way of knowing that, Fannie dear," she said.

"Don't call me *dear,*" Fannie said.

"Where did she die?" Gertrude asked.

"New Orleans." The words seemed to have been ripped from Fannie's mouth; Hattie could almost see them floating in the air.

Louise Phimley looked thoughtful. "Hmm," she mused. "That's an outlandish place. I'll bet she ate a bad clam there. And New Orleans was where she went *after* she deserted you and your father?"

Kicked by a mule. Miss Pat's homely, comical expression jumped into Hattie's head unbidden as she looked at Fannie.

Fannie sputtered. "How—how—"

"Miss Bulkley told my mama all about it," Gertrude announced proudly to the room. "Mama raced up special from the city—she got worried after I wrote her about you coming to school here, Fannie. But Miss Bulkley told Mama that we girls should feel sorry for you, what with your mother eloping like that. *With another man*," she added, leaning forward as if in earnest explanation. "And then dying."

Hattie listened, both horrified and fascinated. Poor Fannie, to have her whole history exposed this way. What might an overly talkative Miss Bulkley say to some nosy parent about her, Hattie?

Sophie nudged her side, as if saying, *See? What did I tell you?* Hattie frowned and withdrew a little into herself.

Carrie Henderson spoke up. "Who cares what Fannie's mother did, or how she died?" she asked, but everyone in the room knew that Carrie was defying Gertrude, not defending Fannie.

Louise sniffed. "Well, I certainly care," she said. "And that girl has the nerve to stand there in her strumpety night-gown, just as good as anyone, and call Minnie Bonesteel a polecat. A polecat!"

Fannie glanced at Hattie again.

Dismayed at being so singled out, Hattie looked away, but her heart seemed to twist. Julie reached over and patted her on the knee. Sophie put an arm around her shoulders, as if protecting her.

"Guttersnipe name-calling," Minnie said with a judicious

air. "Poppy would be furious. But what else can you expect, considering the source? And all because I happened to mention a well-known phenomenon. *Being buried alive,*" she added, in case anyone had forgotten.

"I think I *did* read about something like that in a newspaper once," Lulu Callender said with some relish. She tightened the butterscotch-colored triangle of her folded cashmere shawl around her. "But the article I read was about a man who awoke at his own funeral," she continued. "Why, he sat right up in his coffin and asked for a glass of water!"

Carrie snorted. "I'm glad I don't have his doctor."

"I wonder if the man's wife had already given away his clothes?" practical Julie asked. "She would have had some fast talking to do." She shook her head, smiling sardonically. The curlpapers twisting from her head gave her a look of perpetual surprise.

"I don't know," Lulu said, shrugging. "I never read anything about that."

Minnie cleared her throat. "Well," she said, sounding important, "the Duke of Wellington was worried about being buried alive, I can tell you that. In fact, when he died, they didn't bury him for two whole months."

"Oh, horrible," Mollie gasped, appalled. She looked fascinated, though, and thrilled to be hearing about a real duke—even a dead one.

"Two months is nothing," Carrie scoffed. "Up where we live, in Vermont, folks often have to wait for the thaw before they bury their dead. It's common practice! That's why they build those little stone structures in cemeteries up where the ground stays hard in the winter."

Minnie smoothed her quilt around her knees. "I wouldn't know about that. God has seen fit to *spare* the members of *my* family. His will be done," she added piously, as though quoting Dominie Spencer.

Which she might well be doing, Hattie thought. Rage flared in her chest, but her voice sounded cold when she spoke. "That's a silly brag," she said.

Fannie raised her chin a little, and she flashed Hattie a quick grateful smile.

"What do you mean?" Minnie asked coldly.

"Only that I've read a lot of biographies, and I've noticed that they all end the same way," Hattie said, trying to force her voice into a disinterested drawl.

Mollie giggled nervously, and Julie frowned at Minnie, Hattie's obvious enemy.

Minnie scowled. "You mean the person dies, of course. Well, you're the expert on that, Hattie Knowlton."

Two or three girls drew in their breath; Hattie could hear the sound. "I—I suppose I am," she said, faltering.

Idiot, she told herself. Why didn't you keep your mouth shut?

"Why, when there's a knock on the door," Minnie continued, emboldened, "I'm sure Hattie must think it's the Angel of Death come to call. I don't know why he forgot *you*," she added, pointing at Hattie.

Hattie felt as though she'd been turned to ice. Several girls gasped, and even Louise and Gertrude looked uncomfortable at this remark. Minnie pressed her lips together and flicked her gaze around the room. She seemed to sense that she had gone too far.

Fannie took a step toward Hattie, but then she paused.

"You utter ghoul," Julie said to Minnie. "No wonder no one likes you."

"Plenty of folks like me—at home, anyway, where it counts. But that's not the point," Minnie said as breezily as she could, trying to regain the ground she'd lost. "We were talking about premature burial—and the Duke of Wellington. He died in the summertime, and his family *still* waited two months for the funeral. That's how afraid they were of such a terrible fate as being buried alive."

The room was silent for a moment, each girl's mind busy with the unwelcome thought of a dead person—no matter how beloved—lingering throughout the summer's heat like some ghastly houseguest.

Hattie exhaled silently, relieved that attention had shifted from her to the poor duke.

"Mama once told me that sometimes they bury people with crowbars and shovels in their coffins, *just in case*," Gertrude whispered.

"Or there's always Bateson's Belfry," Minnie said.

"What's Bateson's Belfry?" Louise asked nervously.

Minnie settled back, sure of herself once more. "*Well*, you see, they install an iron bell inside the coffin, and of course there's a cord to ring it with. And they put the cord in the dead person's hand when they bury him. Or *her*," she added, turning to face Fannie once more.

"*Honestly*," Sophie said, shrugging her disdain at this story.

"So, then what?" Julie asked. "All the earthworms for miles around know that a terrible mistake has just been made?"

Minnie sniffed. "Laugh if you will," she said haughtily. "But I hope if *I* die young, which is extremely unlikely, they'll put a cord in my hand."

"We can only hope," Carrie remarked a little ambiguously.

"So tell us, Miss Macintosh," Minnie asked, leaning forward again, "was your poor dead runaway mother holding the cord to Bateson's Belfry in her hand when she was buried? Or at least a shovel, dear?"

"She *said*, don't call her *dear!*" Hattie cried out, pulling away from the warmth of Sophie's arm. She hadn't known she was going to speak until it was too late to take back the words, but this was too much to bear.

Fannie shot her another look in which surprise and gratitude were mingled.

Sophie jabbed Hattie's side again with an unexpectedly sharp elbow, and her blue eyes narrowed in warning.

"Oh, dear, trouble between the cousins," Minnie exclaimed gleefully, looking from Hattie to Sophie. "But it shouldn't exactly astonish you, Sophie, Hattie sticking up for Miss Macintosh this way. *'Like seeks like.'* "

Sophie leaned forward. "Hattie wasn't sticking up for her," she told Minnie hotly. "She was simply stating a fact. We *all* heard Fannie Macintosh ask you not to call her *dear.*"

Mollie and Julie nodded their heads in solemn agreement.

The Quartette was as one, at least in front of the others, but Hattie knew how furious Sophie was to have to defend Fannie, however indirectly.

Hattie's contribution to the conversation had given Fannie new energy. "You little sidewinder," she hissed, looking at Minnie Bonesteel. Her shiny black hair seemed to have gained volume during the fight; it surrounded her head now in wild tangles. "Why, out west," Fannie said, "my papa and I shoot critters like you. Blow them to bits right where they lay."

Fannie has a gun, and she knows how to shoot it, Hattie thought, thrilled.

"I declare," Minnie replied in a lah-di-dah voice. "First I'm a polecat, and now I'm a sidewinder. Which is it to be, Miss Macintosh?"

"A little of both," Fannie said. "You're a rattlesnake with a stink on it, I reckon."

"*I reckon,*" Minnie Bonesteel mocked. "Well," she continued, "I *reckon* you'd better stop trying to push your way into a society that wants nothing to do with you—*or* your father's brand-new money."

"Money can't have an age. It's the same no matter how you make it or how long you've had it," Fannie stated flatly.

"So you say. But at least our mothers didn't run away from us."

"My mother didn't run away from me," Fannie cried, stamping her foot so hard that her hair bounced. "And talk about being buried alive!" she continued. "Why, you girls might as well be dead already for all the living you do. Reciting your little lessons, trotting off to church at the drop of a hat and singing your boring old hymns, and then telling each other how wonderful and exciting everything is."

She was right, Hattie thought—both about how dull the routine was at school and the fact that the girls seemed to cherish it.

"If you hate it so much here, why don't you just leave?" Gertrude asked.

"Because she has nowhere else to go, that's why," Minnie jumped in. "Nobody wants her."

Fannie stalked to the door, and her green gown flowed behind her as if blown by an invisible wind. "You'd better start ringing that coffin bell, *dear,*" she told Minnie over her shoulder. "Not that anyone much worth beans is listening," she added. She flashed a quick, questioning look in Hattie's direction, as if hoping she might follow. Hattie longed to go with her, but she could feel Sophie's fingers digging into her arm.

After a moment Fannie slammed the door behind her. Hattie's heart seemed to twist once more.

"I'll get even with you for that, Miss Macintosh," Minnie Bonesteel whispered. "Oh, indeed I will."

But it was Fannie who had truly had the last word, Hattie reflected with some satisfaction.

≈ 13 ≈

IN FANNIE'S ROOM

Fannie was right, Hattie thought, carefully patting her lips with a napkin after lunch the next day. They *were* being buried alive at Miss Bulkley's. Every day was exactly the same as the one before it.

She refolded the napkin just as she did after every meal and poked it through the beaded napkin ring she'd been issued her very first day—the handiwork of Miss Bulkley herself, Hattie was told. Napkins were laundered only once a week. If she spilled her soup on the tablecloth, Hattie thought, she'd be more likely to attempt to mop it up with her sleeve than to risk Miss Bulkley's wrath by requesting another napkin.

The one o'clock meal had been the usual for a Monday: creamed chicken on soggy toast points, steamed peas, and stewed peaches for dessert. Hattie sighed and looked around. There was no sign of Sophie; she, Mollie, and Julie had finished early and retired to their rooms.

Hattie and Sophie hadn't spoken after leaving Minnie's room the night before, and they'd successfully avoided each other all morning. That had been easy to do, since Sophie did not share Hattie's Monday morning course of study—rhetoric, taken with the younger girls. Hattie had quoted William Shakespeare's *Hamlet* that very morning in class, her finger in the air for the dramatic emphasis Miss Patton loved: *"Be thou as chaste as ice, as pure as snow, thou shalt not escape calumny."*

"But, please, Miss Patton," a worried student had asked, "what *is* calumny, and why can't we escape it?"

"Calumny is slander, Miss Augusta—mean-spirited gossip, that's what it is. And we can't escape it because people can be savage as meat axes," Miss Patton replied, her round cheeks flushed with indignation.

"No matter how good you are?" Augusta's friend Alice asked, quailing.

"No matter," Miss Patton confirmed grimly with one brisk nod. "Why, if you were an *angel* some folks would still find something to slander you with. Now, who's ready with another quotation from the Bard?" she asked, eyeing the troubled little assemblage.

If that's true, why even bother trying to be good? Hattie wondered. Look at the way the girls were treating Fannie, and she hadn't done anything wrong, except to be different.

Though Hattie and Sophie had not spoken, even when

they woke up, dressing instead in chilly silence, Hattie had been aware of being observed almost scientifically by her sharp-eyed cousin—at breakfast, from the hallway. Mollie and Julie had also been watchful. Mollie hung back all morning as if afraid to interfere in the differences between the two girls, and even the usually bold Julie seemed to have withdrawn from her new friend Hattie.

Sophie is showing me who is in charge, Hattie thought, frowning, and the others are going along with it.

Rather than rendering her meek and biddable, though, Sophie's actions were making Hattie angry. Wasn't she more than just an appendage, a shadow to her pretty cousin? Must they agree on *everything*?

In this spirit of rebellion, she did not draw back when Fannie Macintosh stopped her at the dining-room door when lunch was over.

Fannie's hair was pulled back in a chignon style that was almost sedate, compared to the Medusa tangle of the night before, but her attire—an ensemble more suited for evening wear, Hattie thought, with its lavender brocade tunic swaying clear down to her knees—was defiantly cheery. Shiny white silk stockings peeked from under her purple skirt.

"Thanks for sticking up for me last night," Fannie said.

Hattie gave a tiny shrug. "I didn't, not really," she objected—a little regretfully. They moved aside to let the last lunchtime stragglers pass.

"More than anyone else, though," Fannie observed.

"Why does she carry on so?" she asked, not having to bother saying who *she* was.

"I don't know," Hattie replied truthfully. "She took against me, earlier."

"I heard," Fannie said.

Fresh girls and charity cases. Even Fannie knew all about it.

"Oh, let's not pay her no never mind—I think she's just ornery, that's all," Fannie said, putting a tentative hand on Hattie's arm.

"I guess some folks are," Hattie agreed.

Fannie looked suddenly and uncharacteristically shy. "Want to come up to my room for a visit?" she asked, inspecting a spotless black house slipper for dust.

She'd stopped wearing her boots indoors, at least, Hattie noticed. School had taught her that much—but was that a good thing? Hattie gulped. "Well, yes, I would," she said slowly. She usually retired to her own room for a brief rest after luncheon, since the afternoon's activities did not begin until half after two, but her room was Sophie's room, and that's where the others probably were. Perhaps they were even lying in wait, hoping to confront her about her supposed treason the night before!

"I'd *love* to see your room, Miss Macintosh," Hattie said in a much firmer voice. The last girl to arrive at Miss Bulkley's, Fannie had been assigned the belvedere.

"Call me Fannie."

"And call me Hattie."

The two girls climbed silently to the third floor, the domain of the maids and the youngest boarders at Miss Bulkley's. Fannie opened what looked like a closet door and gestured to a steep, uncarpeted staircase. "One more flight of stairs," she said. At the top of the stairs, she pushed open a heavy trapdoor.

Hattie almost gasped, so different was Fannie's small room from any she had seen—in Hammons Mill, Manhattan, or Tarrytown.

At first, it appeared to be all windows—two at the front and back, and one at either side. But Fannie had taken what had clearly been an unused space and turned it into what Hattie imagined Paris, France, and the Wild West might look like if stirred together in a great big bowl.

Sheer curtains had been tacked above each window, giving the room a filmy, dreamlike atmosphere. The paper on the remaining walls was so faded that Hattie couldn't quite make out its design, although she could discern a pale green zigzag that seemed to be tied here and there with wan pink ribbons. But the feeble pattern was no matter, because Fannie had covered most of the small room's walls with decorations of her own.

A full-color poster advertising something called "The Old Glory Blow Out," an event having been celebrated in North Platte, Nebraska, on the Fourth of July, 1882, hung directly over Fannie's narrow bed—a cot like her own, Hattie noted. Nailed boldly to the wall, the poster bragged of prizes to be offered and depicted a cowboy attired in fringe-trimmed trousers. He cradled a gun as tenderly as if it were his beloved. He had long, wavy yellow hair that would be any girl's secret pride, Hattie thought, staring. Indians frolicked behind the man.

"Pa and me were there," Fannie said, nonchalant. "Pa won a rifle."

"Oh," Hattie said, amazed.

A rough, bold-patterned blanket in creams, russets, and browns covered Fannie's little bed. Painted silk pillows rested at the head of the bed, their jeweled colors, depictions of imaginary flowers, and shimmering fringe putting them strangely at odds with the austere woolen bed covering.

An old rocking chair sat in one corner of the room; heaped with clothes, it looked almost as if a person were sitting there, Hattie thought. She gulped, remembering hack driver Mr. Purdy's scary tale about Captain Cobb's wife rocking, rocking, rocking all through the night.

Averting her eyes from the chair, Hattie gazed awestruck around the rest of the room. More nails had been pounded into the walls between the room's many windows, and an impressive array of dresses, wash suits, and glittering gowns hung one to a nail, in plain view.

"This here's my *robe de nuit*," Fanny whispered reverently, lifting a white, embroidery-encrusted dressing gown from a hanger hung alone on one of the nails. Thin cream-colored ribbons fluttered behind it as Fannie removed the gown and swirled it through the air. "Best thing I have. There's even hidden pockets in the lining! Try it on," Fannie urged.

"Oh, no, I—"

"Go ahead," Fannie insisted. "Don't get all skeery on me."

"All right," Hattie said, secretly delighted to have the chance to wear such a garment, even for a moment—finer than anything Aunt Margaret owned, she thought, amazed.

Fannie eased the gown's lace-heavy sleeves over the sober stripes of Hattie's blue-and-black school-day waist. The gown fell clear to Hattie's calves, its thick satin nearly obscuring her black challis skirt. She slipped her hands into the silky pockets.

"Looks pretty," Fannie observed, tilting her head. "Here, take a look," she told Hattie, and she grabbed a small, free-standing oval mirror from a battered dresser and moved it up and down in front of Hattie.

Hattie craned her neck to see. "Wait—hold it there," she said, and the mirror paused midtorso. "Stunning," Hattie said, using one of Aunt Margaret's favorite fashion words, and she turned slightly in an attempt to see the back of the robe.

"It's pretty," Fannie said, looking pleased for Hattie. "The lace is from Bruges, in Belgium. Nuns made it."

"I'd better take it off," Hattie said, and she began to shrug the shimmering dressing gown from her shoulders.

"No hurry," Fannie said, tugging it back in place. "Keep it on a spell. Don't worry, it won't rip or nothing. I wear it every night, studying."

Hattie tried not to goggle at her. She pictured the Quartette at night, each girl wrapped in her mapper against the chill. Their garments were pretty, but also highly serviceable, meant to last the entire school year. They were nothing like this—this *robe de nuit*, this gown of the night.

But it seemed so sad, Hattie thought suddenly—poor Fannie, swanning back and forth across this room, all alone.

"I know it's wrong," Fannie said softly.

"I beg your pardon?" Hattie said, not at all sure what Fannie was referring to.

"I know this gown is wrong for Miss Bulkley's," Fannie said, lifting her chin. "That's why I didn't have it on last night, when—when . . ."

When Minnie Bonesteel savaged you, Hattie thought.

"She sent that *Miss Phimley* up to fetch me," Fannie said with disgust, exactly as if she had read Hattie's mind. "But all my clothes are wrong," she said. "Not like yours," she added, giving Hattie a sideways glance.

Hattie's finger traced the sinuous line of a nun-embroidered willow leaf before she decided to speak. "If my clothes are right," she said, "it's only because Aunt Margaret chose them for me. If I'd come to Miss Bulkley's straight from Hammons Mill, why, they'd have told me that tradespeople must enter through the back door, that's all."

Cool relief washed over Hattie like summer rain as she said these words. Finally, there was someone to whom she could speak the truth—without shame!

Fannie smiled at Hattie, as if thanking her for this confidence. "Wish I had an Aunt Margaret to tell me what to wear," she finally said.

"No, you don't," Hattie said, laughing.

"Yes, I do."

"Well, who chose your outfits, then?" Hattie asked, abandoning the Aunt Margaret debate.

"Friend of Pa's," Fannie said shortly. "She lives in Manhattan. She likes things fancy," she added. She walked back to her bureau, setting the mirror on its crowded surface.

Hattie followed her. "What are those?" she asked shyly, pointing to three papery-looking objects that sat on a chipped china plate like ancient hors d'oeuvres.

"Rattles," Fannie said with a sudden grin.

"Do you mean like *baby* rattles?" Hattie asked, surprised, leaning forward to examine them more closely. They looked handcrafted, almost, each made up of a series of translucent rings, tapered from large to small.

Fannie laughed aloud; it was a silvery sound that Hattie realized she hadn't heard before. "No, silly," Fannie said, "*sidewinder* rattles. You know, rattlesnakes." She wiggled an index finger in the air as if demonstrating something.

Hattie had been about to touch one of the rattles, but she jerked her finger back when she heard Fannie's explanation. "Are they poisonous?" she asked, eyeing them nervously.

"No," Fannie reassured her. "It's the poison in the fangs that kills you. *Slow*," she added, relishing the word. "Here, hold one," Fannie said, and she took the smallest rattle from the plate and placed it in Hattie's suddenly clammy hand.

"How—how did you come by this?" Hattie asked, holding her hand as flat as if she were feeding an apple to a bad-tempered horse. The rattle was light and dry.

"Pa shot it, then we frizzled it up and et it. Tasted pretty good, too," Fannie added, clearly enjoying Hattie's reaction.

"Wasn't this one just a baby?"

"Yep," Fannie confirmed, "but they're the worst for poison. Don't know why." Fannie removed the rattle, and Hattie rubbed her hand furtively against the cool satin robe.

"Want something to eat?" Fannie asked. "Pa's friend is better with food than she is about clothes," she continued. "She's sent me hard pretzels and macaroons and candy and—"

"Why, I'd love to," Hattie said, and they settled happily onto Fannie's blanket.

"You know, it's a funny thing," Fannie said conversationally, opening a box she pulled out from under her cot, "but sometimes at night, that old rocker just starts a-moving on its own."

"It *does?*" Hattie squeaked.

Fannie pointed at her and burst out laughing. "Got you good, I did!" she crowed. "You should see your face. Don't go getting the vapors on me, now."

"*Fannie,*" Hattie said, clutching her chest dramatically.

"For heaven's sake—you scared me half to death. So, Mr. Purdy told you his scary tale, too?"

"He must tell everyone," Fannie said, subsiding. She offered Hattie a box of sugar-coated nougat. "It's his party piece, I reckon. Not that I don't believe in ghosts, mind. 'Specially out west, 'specially in Virginia City. Oh, I could tell you *tales*—I got a hundred of 'em."

"Tales about ghosts?" Hattie popped a nougat in her mouth and licked her fingers clean.

Fannie nodded. "Why, I seen three of them myself." She reached for a piece of candy.

"I don't know if I—"

"The first thing is," Fannie interrupted smoothly, "they're not like you think—all clanky with chains and howling and all. No, not at all."

"What *are* they like?" Hattie asked in spite of herself.

"Well," Fannie said, "the first ghost I ever saw was this old miner who lived at the same hotel as Pa and me. He was killed in a cave-in. They found his body and all, and buried him, too. But then I saw him—about a week later."

"You *did*?"

Fannie nodded, solemn. "I was walking by his room at the hotel. They'd packed up his things, see, and they'd just done cleaning the place out, so it was good and empty. But there he was, sitting on the bed and cleaning his boots. He looked up at me and winked."

"*No*," Hattie said, enthralled.

"Next ghost, I saw reflected in a mirror," Fannie continued, as matter-of-fact as if she were describing real people she had known. "We had rooms on the second floor, see, and there was this balcony running clear across the front of the hotel, just outside. So you could see the gunfights better."

"*Gunfights?*"

Fannie nodded. "And I was brushing my hair one morning, looking in the mirror, and I could see this lady walk in front of my window—wearing a long white veil. But when I turned to look out the window, there was no one there."

"Who was it, do you think?" Hattie asked.

"A bride who'd been jilted—ten years earlier. She died after that. That's what I heard, anyhow."

"What about the third ghost?"

Fannie looked down for a moment, then said, "That one was my mama."

The very dust motes seemed to freeze in midair as Hattie waited for her to continue. "Did she appear to you in a vision?" Hattie finally asked.

Fannie gave her a twisted, heartbreaking smile. "No, that would have been seeing an angel. I said I saw a *ghost*. There's a difference, you know. I didn't even know she was dead, the time it happened," she continued. "I just thought she was *gone*. But then I woke up one morning, early, and there she was—all dressed up, and looking out the window. Like she was waiting for someone."

Shivers crept up Hattie's arms. She didn't want little Joey to be a ghost.

"So, see," Fannie concluded, her tone lightening, "I think ghosts are just stuck, like. Stuck waiting for someone or cleaning their boots or something homely like that. But *forever*," she added, grinning suddenly.

"Why, Fannie Macintosh," Hattie said, angry and relieved at the same time, "I believe you made those stories up, didn't you? *Didn't you?*"

"I reckon," she said with a wink. "All but one of them, anyway."

"Which one?" Hattie asked, her heart skidding once more.

But Fannie wouldn't say.

It was as though Sophie, Mollie, and Julie had conspired to win Hattie back to the Quartette by showering her with attentions too tender to resist. "Oh, *there* you are," Julie said, linking her arm through Hattie's as she and Fannie walked down the main stairs and through the annex door on their way to afternoon classes. "We decided that we should all draw fruit this afternoon," she announced gaily.

"Lovely apples," Sophie added, imitating Miss Brownback's refined voice. "And then we'll play croquet. Just us four."

"I'll demolish you all," Julie said.

"They're awaiting you in chorus, Miss Macintosh," Mollie told Fannie quite kindly. She took Hattie's other arm in her own, and she and Julie walked her to the drawing classroom, with Sophie leading the way.

Fannie was left standing alone.

Hattie didn't even have a chance to look back, it all happened so fast.

~ 14 ~

WHY DO YOU CARE?

s Lulu going to be all right?" Hattie asked Sophie late the next evening, laying down her pen. It had been a long, troubling day.

Seated on her bed, Sophie yawned, reminding Hattie of a sleepy kitten. "According to the doctor she will be," she said, but she sounded skeptical.

"What actually happened?" Hattie asked.

Sophie looked up, a tragic expression on her face. "Her leg got burned," she said. "Now Lulu's *flawed.*"

"Flawed?" Hattie asked. The word seemed to sting. That was exactly the way *she* felt, Hattie realized: flawed, marred, damaged by the tragedies that had befallen her.

All the more reason to keep quiet about them, Hattie thought, and to be grateful to the Quartette for accepting her without question. She should be glad they'd silently forgiven her for visiting Fannie's room.

Hattie tried not to think about Fannie—who had, after all, confided in her, thinking they were friends.

All right, they'd confided in *each other*. She had said things to Fannie she couldn't say to anyone else.

And they'd had fun, she admitted to herself.

"Lulu is flawed now," Sophie repeated. "There will likely be a scar."

"But—but who would ever see such a thing?" Hattie asked.

Sophie pressed her lips together, as if trying to keep a secret, but then she spoke. "Her husband might," she said.

"Oh, Soph," Hattie said, attempting a laugh, "I don't think that's very likely." She tried—and failed—to imagine Aunt Margaret showing Uncle Charley her limbs.

Sophie shook her head as if she knew things about married life that Hattie could only guess at. "It might happen," she finally said.

Both girls were quiet for a moment. Hattie stifled a yawn of her own; Miss Bulkley's girls had gotten very little sleep the night before. Only moments after midnight, the cry had sounded: *"Fire!"*

"We could have all been killed last night," Sophie told Hattie in a matter-of-fact voice. She started brushing her hair, counting under her breath.

"But we weren't," Hattie pointed out.

Sophie kept brushing. "In a way," she said thoughtfully, "this is all Fannie Macintosh's fault, isn't it?" She paused, trying for it to seem as though bringing up Fannie's name was a natural, logical thing to do—as though she and Hattie had never even mentioned the girl before.

Hattie didn't say a word. Sophie was like a cat, not a kitten, she thought warily; her cousin watched her with ferocious eyes, invisible tail thrashing. It was as though Sophie was waiting to pounce upon Hattie, the hapless mouse.

The only safe thing to do was to be still.

"Twenty-seven, twenty-eight," Sophie said before pausing in her brushing. "I mean," she explained patiently, "if Fannie hadn't come to Miss Bulkley's, then Lulu wouldn't have stayed up late writing to her mama about her, would she?"

Hattie felt her jaw sag. Sophie was unbelievable.

"Twenty-nine, thirty. And if Lulu hadn't stayed up late," Sophie continued in a voice of pure reason, "then she wouldn't have gotten so sleepy. And if Lulu hadn't been so sleepy, why, she would have been more careful with her lamp! *Thirty-one, thirty-two."*

Hattie felt as though she had to catch her breath, she was so startled. "I don't see how you can say this is Fannie's fault," she finally said.

"I don't see how you can say it isn't," Sophie shot back. *"Thirty-five, thirty-six.* And now," she added, "perhaps Lulu's chances are spoiled."

"Lulu's chances for *what?"* Hattie asked.

"For marital bliss," Sophie said. *"Thirty-nine, forty.* It's all Fannie's fault."

"Oh, Soph—why do you hate Fannie so?" Hattie cried, breaking her silence about the girl. "Why do you care?"

Sophie threw down her brush. "Well, why do you like her so much, Hattie? That's what I want to know. A girl like that! And after all I've done for you, too," she added with a sniff.

"But—but Sophie," Hattie sputtered, "I appreciate all the things that you've done—and your family, too. How could I not? But I can't keep thanking you and thanking you—or else I'd never get any sleep," she said, attempting a small joke.

Sophie didn't laugh.

"Anyway," Hattie added hastily, "I don't see what that has to do with Fannie."

"I already explained it to you once," Sophie said, impatient. "A girl has to choose her friends carefully. Why, I've chosen you, haven't I?" She smiled, as if willing her cousin to see her reasoning.

Hattie jumped to her feet and started pacing. Sophie watched her.

"But I don't understand it, Soph—why can't we simply decide to disagree about this one little thing? We can like different people, can't we?"

Sophie seemed to think about this, then she shook her head, her dark blue eyes serious. "There's more to it than that, Hattie. Why would you defy me this way?"

Hattie was astonished. "*Defy* you?" she asked.

Sophie nodded. "You know that I don't like Fannie Macintosh," she explained. "That ought to be reason enough for you to shun her, if you had any loyalty to me."

"I *am* loyal to you," Hattie protested hotly.

"Well, prove it, then."

Hattie stared at her cousin. "You have everything, Soph," she said at last. "You have parents and money and you're beautiful, too. Fannie has nothing." And I have nothing, either, Hattie thought. Not compared to Sophie Hubbard, anyway.

"You think I'm beautiful?" Sophie asked, momentarily distracted.

"You know you are," Hattie told her. "So why can't you leave Fannie alone?"

Sophie narrowed her eyes. "I don't want her to have you," she said. "You're *my* cousin and *my* friend."

"But—but you don't mind it that I'm friends with Julie and Mollie, do you?"

"That's not the same," Sophie said. "I chose them for you."

"Why does *that* make a difference?"

"Because Julie and Mollie are like us," Sophie said. She stood up. "Fannie's just plain pushy, that's what! She's pushy and flashy and you never know what she's going to say next."

I *like* that about her, Hattie thought, rebellion stirring anew in her heart.

Sophie smiled and reached out her hand to Hattie. "Come," she said, coaxing, and—as if pulled by a magnet—

Hattie walked across the room to Sophie. "Let's sit," Sophie said, and she and Hattie perched gingerly on Sophie's untidy bed.

The two girls looked at each other, and then Sophie burst into giggles. "Can you believe how funny Miss Bulkley looked in her nightgown last night?" she asked, making it clear the argument was over—for now at least. For her part, Hattie was glad not to talk about Fannie. It was easier to simply let Sophie take charge.

"I—I—I didn't know there was that much sprigged flannel in the *world*," Hattie finally managed to say.

"She was brave, though," Sophie reminisced. "She was quite a heroine, wrapping Lulu in that quilt the way she did."

"You were a heroine, too," Hattie offered, wanting to flatter her cousin, "saving Miss Brownback's false hair the way you did."

"I always knew she wore a hairpiece—and a nice one, too," Sophie said, nodding sagely. "Mama has enough of them, so I should know. Why," she continued, "when I was little, her dressing room used to scare me, there were so many heads of hair in it—enough for three or four mamas, I used to think. I wondered what had happened to all those women, that my mama had their hair."

"You were brave, Soph," Hattie told her cousin again, trying to put a seal upon their unspoken truce. "That hair looked like a flag streaming behind you when you ran down the stairs."

Sophie looked doubtful. "I didn't think about what I was doing before I did it. Is that really being brave?"

Hattie knew Sophie was pressing her to repeat the compliment, and she didn't hesitate. "Why, it certainly is."

Just as a person can think about what she is doing and still be cowardly, Hattie added bitterly to herself. She crossed to her desk again and picked up her pen. No writing about Fannie Macintosh tonight, she told herself—her confused feelings about loyalty and friendship would have to remain in her head, where they were truly private.

> *Last night we had quite a little excitement, Miss Lulu Callender being the designer and special artist of it. She rooms alone this year, and by pushing her gas light into her curtain made a grand illumination for us.*
>
> *Several of the inmates of this establishment distinguished themselves, Miss Bulkley by extinguishing the fire and Lulu's dress. Kind Sophie, may her name be covered with glory, saved from water, fire, and other destructive powers* <u>*Miss Brownback's switch.*</u>

TEA WITH THE SPENCERS

The reluctant tea goers crunched noisily through the fallen leaves on the croquet lawn, ringed on three sides by Miss Bulkley's now-empty cutting garden.

"Mind the spiderwebs," Miss Patton called out as the girls in the little group walked through the gap in the tall hedge, arms waving in front of them. "I think Miss Brownback already bore the brunt of those webs," Hattie observed—to no one in particular.

They walked next through the clothes-drying area. Empty, the maze of lines overhead cast long snaky shadows on faded grass. Next, the teagoers passed the remains of last summer's vegetable garden, heaped now with rows of hay.

Miss Bulkley's property was a full block deep, and the final part of their trek through the rear yard took them through a wild, frost-bitten tangle of brush at the very end of the garden. "I hate this shortcut," Gertrude moaned as a wet branch snapped against her cloak. Miss Patton pushed open a rain-swollen gate and the party stepped onto John Street.

A cold, wet November wind whipped the girls' cloaks against their ankles as they plodded along behind the Misses Patton and Brownback. Leaves sailed by like tiny kites. In front of Hattie, a damp oak leaf landed on Fannie Macintosh's shoulder and stuck there like a military decoration.

Hattie hadn't spoken to Fannie in two days now. There hadn't really been *time*, she kept telling herself, what with classes and the Quartette.

But she knew better, deep down, and so did Fannie Macintosh, by gosh.

Fannie had approached her once in the school annex washing room, but Fannie didn't know that Sophie was using a chamber pot just behind the screen. Aware of her cousin's presence, Hattie turned away, busying herself at the sink.

When she looked up, Fannie was gone.

Coward, Hattie berated herself once more.

Mealtimes, classrooms, hallways: Miss Bulkley's girls seemed to flow through the school like water, mingling and murmuring. But it was not necessary for Hattie to *actively* avoid Fannie; it was as though Hattie had become invisible to the wild girl.

Fannie seemed not to take much notice of anyone any

longer, in fact. In a mere two days, she had lost much of her energy and verve, her very wildness. If she were a teakettle, Hattie thought, one might even say that some hand had turned the heat down under her. Hattie felt guilty, because that hand might have been hers.

Everyone had noticed the difference. "I think our dear Miss Macintosh has been quelled. She has been tamed," Sophie announced to the Quartette only a few hours earlier. She had spoken with a great deal of satisfaction, but none of them could think what to say after that. Who was there to complain about now? A tamed Fannie was a dull Fannie, and a dull Fannie was almost worse than no Fannie at all. Or so Hattie couldn't help thinking—if a little confusedly.

But then, she was trying hard not to think much about Fannie.

"March on, ladies. Let's see some grit!" Miss Patton cried gaily, turning around for a moment. Her round face gleamed like a beacon beneath the broad felt curve of her best autumn hat. Three turkey feathers arose from its encircling ribbon like large exclamation points.

Fannie, Hattie, Gertrude, and Daisy—all the new girls at Miss Bulkley's—trudged along behind the new teachers, bidden to tea with the Spencers. New congregants meeting with new clergy was one of Reverend Todd's eccentric concoctions and was probably resented equally by all participants, Hattie thought grimly.

She knew *she* resented it. But then, the Spencers had

already done their worst. Even Sophie conceded this, privately, to Hattie. "Just don't let them go into any *detail*," she pleaded, knowing that Gertrude, at least, would eagerly carry back any teatime gossip.

A grocery wagon clattered by as they crossed the street near the post office, and its big wheels sent gobs of mud flying to each side of the road. "There's some grit for you," Hattie muttered, jumping back just in time.

"Almost there," Miss Patton sang out, leading the damp and straggly line around a curve to Orchard Street, where the church had rented as large a house as they could find for the numerous Spencers.

"I'm freezing," Gertrude whined behind Hattie. "Also, I think I'm getting a sore throat. That could be *dangerous*." She coughed a little, as if auditioning for the doctor, and then she stumbled, trying to keep up. "It's so muddy," her complaint continued. "And it's icy mud. We should have taken a hack, that's what we should have done. Why, at home, we always take hacks, no matter how short the distance—or if it's just us children, we go in our donkey cart. It's so jolly, and Mama wraps us all up tight in a buffalo robe, and we're warm as—as—"

". . . as horse poop," Hattie heard Fannie say.

Hattie almost choked on swallowed laughter. Perhaps Fannie was regaining some of her spirit!

Neither Miss Patton nor Miss Brownback turned around, but Hattie thought she saw their shoulders shake with mirth. "*Simile*," Hattie overheard Miss Brownback observe to her fellow teacher.

"What?" Gertrude squealed, unable to believe her ears. "What nasty thing did you say to me, Fannie Macintosh? I'm telling!"

Fannie turned around and shrugged her innocence, not meeting Hattie's eye, and the leaf on her shoulder blew away.

"I think she said you're as warm as a horseshoe," Daisy called out from the end of the line.

"That's right," Hattie lied, although *as warm as a horseshoe* didn't seem to make much sense—unless the horseshoe was hot off the forge, and then it would be very warm, indeed.

She drew her plush green cloak close around her and forced herself to stare at Fannie's back as they plodded along, dodging puddles and sidestepping fallen branches. In a show of bravado that took Hattie's breath away, Fannie had appeared in a long hooded cape of such blinding crimson wool, and of such a sweepingly pretty cut, that the little girls passing through the front hall rushed up to her, exclaiming their admiration and fingering its soft weave.

They weren't yet aware that Fannie was being shunned.

Fannie had met Hattie's eye, lifted her chin proudly— and then turned away.

"They're here," a boy's voice called out, and he ran off toward the house to alert his mother. Two littler Spencer boys stopped swinging on a sagging gate long enough to gape at the parade their tea guests made.

"The circus is in town," Miss Brownback called out, referring, of course, to their own arrival.

"The circus is in town!" the little boys echoed joyfully. They clasped each other in miniature bear hugs and jumped up and down in the icy mud.

"No, wait," Miss Brownback said weakly, "I didn't mean—"

But it was too late; the children had run off to tell their brothers the wonderful news. "We'll be pretty sour apples after *that* gets sorted out," Miss Patton observed with a wry chuckle.

The Spencers' house was white, though in need of a fresh coat of paint, and slightly shabby, but it had a boxy respectability that far surpassed the crowded little house the family had inhabited in Hammons Mill.

They'd come up in the world, Hattie thought—just as she had.

Mrs. Spencer was waiting for them on the front porch. She was wringing her hands, but she tried to welcome her guests with a smile. "Oh," she said as they approached, "I don't know where the Dominie is—he was supposed to be home by now. I've sent Abel off to search for him."

Abel Spencer couldn't find his nose with his eyes shut, Hattie thought, remembering the boy. Not that a bloodhound would do much better. Dominie Spencer was up to his old tricks, leaving his wife to do all the work.

They wouldn't lay eyes on *him* this afternoon—not at so humble an event.

And Mrs. Spencer wasn't looking at all well, not in Hattie's opinion. Attired neatly enough, although wearing an out-of-date princess dress that strained at the seams in spite of the usual looseness of the style, Mrs. Spencer looked wan and tired. She gripped her back for a moment as though it pained her. She exchanged shy hellos with Hattie, however, and gave her hand an especially warm squeeze in greeting. "I've missed you, my dear," she murmured.

"I—I've missed you, too," Hattie said, surprised to find that she meant it, for Mrs. Spencer reminded her of home.

In the Spencers' tobacco brown parlor, six boys stood at attention in order of size, as if ready for battle. The littlest two—the gate swingers—had tear-stained faces, Hattie noticed, although one of them suddenly seemed to recognize Hattie. He waggled his fingers at her in greeting.

He had come to play with Joey once, Hattie thought, shocked at this unexpected memory. She gave him a wave in return.

The youngest Spencer stared at Miss Brownback with undisguised hatred. He must have heard that the circus was *not* in town, Hattie thought, feeling a little sorry for the boy. Abijah, she thought his name was.

"Oh, dear," Miss Brownback said.

"Yes! Well!" Mrs. Spencer said, wringing her hands again. "Arthur, take the ladies' cloaks, would you? And Alonzo, go tell Nell that we're ready for tea, now."

"Are you Red Riding Hood?" Arthur asked as he gazed at Fannie.

"No—I'm the wicked wolf," Fannie replied, flashing a terrible grin in his direction.

After he'd been calmed down, Arthur staggered off, trailing an armload of heavy wool. Fannie's cloak glowed red in pride of place atop the others. Alonzo disappeared to search for Nell, the hired girl, and everyone else sat down.

The Spencer boys goggled at their guests, and Mrs. Spencer closed her eyes for a moment.

No one spoke.

"I'll tell you what," Miss Patton said, breaking the uncomfortable silence. She leaned forward, as if about to tell the Spencer boys a secret. Hattie was amused to see the boys lean forward, too. "Are you lads familiar with Washington Irving's famous story 'Rip Van Winkle'?"

The older boys nodded, and then the younger ones did, too. "She called us *lads*," one of them whispered.

"Washington Irving lived near here!" Arthur said, returning to the room empty-handed. "Must have been a neighbor, I reckon."

"Mr. Irving did live in Tarrytown, but at Sunnyside, down by the river," Miss Patton said, "and that would have been some years back. As you recall, though," she continued, "Rip Van Winkle fell asleep for twenty years. That was quite a little nap," she added jokily.

"He took it in our backyard," one of the boys asserted.

Amos, Hattie thought his name was—the one who had played with Joey.

A smaller brother stared at Amos admiringly, and Hattie suppressed a giggle. Fannie was looking amused, too, she noticed.

"Well, no," Miss Patton interjected. "Rip Van Winkle fell asleep up around Palenville, as a matter of fact. It's in the mountains—not far from here, though. Just across the river and up north a distance."

"Do tell! I've been there," Mrs. Spencer said, her cares momentarily forgotten.

"I thought it was just a story," Arthur objected hotly.

"Beg pardon?" Miss Patton said, startled.

"How could a story man fall asleep in a real place?" Arthur asked. "Can't be!"

"Arthur," Mrs. Spencer scolded. "Apologize to the lady."

"Won't," a rebellious Arthur replied, jutting out his chin.

There was a clatter from the hallway, and Hattie heard a muffled exclamation. That must be poor Nell, she thought. Hattie remembered the Spencers' long-suffering hired girl from the old days in Hammons Mill.

"No need to apologize, little boy," Miss Patton said hurriedly. "Why, that wasn't even the point of my tale. I was going to say that six hundred years before Jesus was born, there was *another* Rip Van Winkle–type character in literary history. His name was Epimenides, and he lived on the island of Crete. But he fell asleep for fifty years!"

"*That* was in our backyard," Amos said proudly.

A snort of laughter escaped Fannie, and Hattie hid a grin.

"I memember," the youngest Spencer said, nodding wisely as he stumbled over the word.

Miss Patton sighed; her story was obviously both over— and unappreciated. She made a tiny shrug in Miss Brownback's direction. *I tried,* it seemed to say.

Mrs. Spencer moaned as if the burdens of the afternoon had become too much for her.

"*I'll* tell you what," Fannie Macintosh said. Hattie saw her catch her hostess's eye and wink sympathetically before the silence descended again. She leaned forward just as Miss Pat had done a few minutes earlier, and some of her old sparkle was definitely back.

Hattie's heart thudded. Who knew *what* Fannie was going to say? She decided she could barely wait to hear.

"What?" Amos asked, sounding skeptical.

"Well, it's a story about the transcontinental railroad," Fannie said, drawing the words out in a tantalizing way.

Mrs. Spencer flushed with excitement. "I've heard they have parlor cars," she exclaimed.

Fannie nodded. "That's right, ma'am, they do. And you can get all sorts of delicious things to eat in a parlor car."

"Like what?" a hungry Spencer boy asked.

"Oh, like strawberries and cream, for instance," Fannie told him, nonchalant.

"I've et that," Arthur announced.

"Where's tea?" Amos asked, looking around.

"And there are sleeping cars, too," Fannie continued unperturbed. "But you can get bumped around something fierce in those. Why, I fell out of bed on a train once and landed smack on the floor in a car full of soldiers and cowboys. And to pile on the agony, I wasn't even wearing my prettiest nightgown. I swear! I was mad enough to swallow a horny toad backwards."

If Fannie's intention had been to create a small sensation, she succeeded. Whether it was the news that she had ridden on a train, fallen out of bed on a train, been seen—not merely by the general public, but by soldiers and cowboys!—wearing her second-best nightgown on a train, or practically sworn in a preacher's own parlor that impressed her various listeners, Hattie couldn't tell. But impressed they were.

Or perhaps it was the horny toad that did it.

"Goodness," Miss Brownback said.

"Cowboys!" Abijah Spencer shouted.

"What sort of nightgown was it?" Daisy wanted to know.

"No one is ever going to believe this," Gertrude stated. She peered around the sitting room as if searching for witnesses who would back her up when she told the story later—which she most certainly would, Hattie knew.

"Was the train in a terrible bloody wreck, miss?" Amos asked hopefully.

"I swear!" the youngest Spencer repeated clearly and with great enthusiasm, and Mrs. Spencer didn't even scold him, so astonished was she at the thrilling turn her dull little party had taken.

At that moment Hattie saw how lonely the woman must be—married to the awful Dominie and stranded in a brand-new town with seven little boys. How difficult it must be for her simply to get through each day, much less to obey the whim of her husband and give a successful tea party for a bunch of strangers.

It had taken Hattie years to achieve this understanding; Fannie had realized it in five minutes.

She had never been more impressed by Fannie than she was at that moment.

The parlor door banged open, and Nell pushed her way into the room holding an immense tray stacked high with cups and saucers. "Tea's on the way," she announced, and Hattie's eyes flew to the still-swinging door. She half expected to see a huge teapot stride into the Spencers' parlor on stubby little legs, so strange had the afternoon been thus far.

"Did I ever tell you about the time I et a rattlesnake?" Fannie asked the room conversationally.

"*Oh!*" Mrs. Spencer said, gasping, and she started from her chair.

Last night Mrs. Spencer presented her husband with a son. Number 8.

I think with Miss Brownback that the Dominie had better stop filling up his house with boys by trying to get a girl . . .

RHUBARB

*T*wo days passed. Fannie and Hattie didn't speak, although Hattie wanted to approach Fannie several times. But Hattie felt almost paralyzed by the stepped-up attentions of the Quartette. "Brush my hair, would you?" Sophie might ask if Hattie started to look restless midafternoon.

"Help me to conjugate these verbs," Julie would say in her commanding way.

"Wait until you hear what happened to Anne next," Mollie might announce breathlessly, late at night, speaking of Miss Woolson's book. "She is reunited with her lost love!"

Anyway, Hattie thought, perhaps Fannie doesn't want to talk to *me*. Why would she?

At dinner, Fannie poked at her rhubarb-pear crumble— a special Sunday treat—with some suspicion. "Is this celery, or what?" she asked, making a face. "We don't have such a nasty thing out west." She seemed to have regained some of her confidence since her performance at the Spencers' tea party—and without any help from Hattie. "The Spencers probably would have named that baby for me if it had been a girl," she had announced at one point.

Hattie opened her mouth to answer, but Gertrude Spesh spoke first. "That new girl doesn't even know what rhubarb is," she announced to those seated around her, in case they'd missed Fannie's comment. Gertrude spoke quietly, although most of the teachers had already excused themselves from the table, having afternoon plans of their own. The girls were allowed to linger at the dining table on Sundays.

"I'm not new anymore, and my name is Fannie Macintosh, as you very well know," Fannie told Gertrude.

"Fannie Macintosh is crazy for boys," Gertrude elaborated to the others. "And she talks all the time, and she doesn't know what rhubarb is." She lifted a forkful of the stringy dessert daintily to her own mouth, as if showing a savage Fannie Macintosh how these things should be done.

"Not everyone eats rhubarb," Carrie Henderson said, instantly opposing her roommate.

"That's right," Hattie concurred, wanting to show Fannie—what? Loyalty? But almost immediately, she found herself glancing nervously at Sophie. Sophie avoided her eyes.

"Normal people do," Minnie Bonesteel snapped.

Minnie had never supported Gertrude in an argument before. Gertrude flashed Minnie a quick look of gratitude and, with new confidence, adjusted the woolen shawl she'd wrapped twice around her neck and secured with a cameo brooch her mother had given her. "People from the land of steady habits eat rhubarb all the time," she said, as if making an announcement. "It's a favorite of ours."

Fannie put down her fork. "'The land of steady habits'?" she asked. "What's that supposed to be?"

"My mama says it's *here*, or nearabouts," Gertrude said, as if explaining where the center of the universe was. She put her palms gently on the edge of the table as she spoke, and she leaned forward. "New England," she added in a solemn voice, seeing Fannie's baffled expression.

Fannie shrugged and gave a careless smile to the girls who were staring at her, waiting to see her reaction. She fluffed the peacock satin ruffles that framed her neck. "Oh," she said. "No need to get all wrathy on me just because I'm a little particular about what I eat."

Hattie couldn't help giggling at that, and this time Sophie did stare at her. It was not a friendly look.

Gertrude and Minnie exchanged outraged glances at Fannie's proud words, but Lulu Callender—quite recovered from the fire, and promised to be mending without a permanent scar, after all—looked fascinated. "What do *you* like to eat for a sweetie?" she asked, and she, Lydia, and Daisy leaned forward as one to hear Fannie's answer.

"She eats candied buffalo bits," Minnie Bonesteel said, as if answering a test question aloud.

"Prairie dog meringues," Louise Phimley suggested gleefully.

Gertrude thought hard, desperate to add something to this exchange. "Fannie likes elephant eclairs!" she finally said. Delighted with her own wit, her light brown eyes flashed with malice beneath the pale lashes that encircled them.

"They don't have elephants in the pioneer west," Carrie said, pleased to best Gertrude in any way that she could. "They're only in Mr. Barnum's circus, silly. I saw one just last summer, in Brooklyn."

Behind her, Gladys dropped a tray of dirty silverware, astonished.

"You *did*?" Daisy squealed above the clatter. Lydia Gilbert shook her head, impressed.

Carrie nodded. "It lifted up a person with its nose," she told them.

"Huh," Gertrude said, obviously doubting her—but afraid to say so directly.

"I like peppermint cake," Fannie said, "with fudge icing. That's my favorite."

Peppermint cake with fudge icing was the perfect dessert for Fannie Macintosh, Hattie thought, having had it once the previous spring. The cake was spicy and sweet at the same time, and, once introduced to it, you never forgot it.

But a furtive look at Sophie kept the comment from escaping her lips.

Minnie shook her head impatiently. "Well, favorite desserts are not even what we were talking about," she said. "Not in the first place. You were telling us how we should be husband hunting already, that's what you were saying."

"And it's the simple truth," Fannie repeated. "If getting married is to be a girl's fate, then it only makes sense that the girl should be the one to do the choosing. You should control what you can of your future! And a girl had better choose right and start looking early. Because when she says *yes* to a young man, well—that's her whole entire life." She tried to tuck a wayward curl behind her ear.

Fannie was right, Hattie thought. Why, look at poor Mrs. Spencer!

"But we're just girls, yet," Minnie said, leaning forward to make her point. "Only immigrants get married when they're as young as we are."

"I'm not saying we should marry *now*," Fannie said scornfully. "I'm only saying that any smart girl of sixteen or older is already looking. I'm fifteen and a half, and I know *I* certainly plan to start soon."

Minnie pushed back her chair and arose majestically. Louise and Gertrude stood up, too, as if attached to Minnie by invisible wires. "You've made that abundantly clear, Miss Macintosh," Minnie said. "You have interrogated each and every one of us about our older brothers, and you probably already know the name of every boy within a three-block radius of the school. But frankly," she continued, "I don't care to listen to any more disgusting details of your scheming. It was bad enough seeing you ogle every male over the age of thirteen in church—even the little Spencer lads, I'll wager."

"Oh, come on, Minnie. What Fannie's saying is not so different from the things you were telling us last month," Hattie heard herself say.

Hattie could almost *feel* her cousin's eyes on her. Oh, no, she thought.

Minnie paused halfway to the door. "I beg your pardon?" she said, turning around to glare at Hattie.

Hattie ignored Sophie. "You were telling us that we should only have to study things here that would help us when we got married," she said, trying to keep the wobble out of her voice.

"That makes sense," Fannie observed, nodding her agreement. A few black curls sprang loose again from their confines.

"Shut your mouth," Minnie yelled, whirling to face her once more. "Don't you dare agree with me! I have no intention of marrying some—some no-account cowboy. And that's the best that you can ever hope for, *Miss Macintosh.*"

Minnie uttered Fannie's last name as if it was a swearword, but Fannie simply laughed at her. "Shut my *mouth*?

Oh, that's nice ladylike talk! Reminds me of what my pa told me once," she added, a stagey, reminiscent look on her face. "He said, 'You should never fight with a skunk, Fannie—because you'll both get stink on you, but the skunk likes it.' So don't you try that shouting bunkum on me, Minnie Bonesteel," she concluded. "I wasn't born in the woods to be scared by an owl."

Two or three girls were giggling by now, in spite of themselves—including Hattie, who thought that Fannie was probably exaggerating her folksiness to further enrage Minnie.

"But you *were* born in the woods," Minnie snapped. "And that's the point." She shot Louise and Gertrude a look of triumph and the three swept from the dining room.

Fannie was undaunted, though. "Each of us had to be born someplace."

She sounded surprisingly philosophical, Hattie thought. "That's right," she concurred softly, thinking of herself as well as of Fannie.

Fannie flashed her a look of gratitude. "It's not as though I grew in the ground like a potato," she continued, bold as she had ever been. "So I'm *not* a member of the cod-fish aristocracy," she added, eyeing the few girls who were still scattered around the long dining table. "I can survive knowing that."

"What's 'the codfish aristocracy'?" Mollie whispered to Sophie.

"She means us, I suppose," Sophie said in a cool, clear voice, "people whose families made their fortunes in business on the East Coast. Vulgar moneybags," she explained.

"But—but how else would a person make money?" Mollie asked, confused.

"My papa inherited his," Lulu announced. "And Lydia's family has always been rich. But my grandpapa was a—a codfish, I suppose," she added, looking a little sorry to admit it. "*He* was in business."

Fannie looked uncomfortable. "I didn't mean there was anything wrong with working to make money," she said.

"I should hope not!" Sophie said, scraping her chair back from the table with unaccustomed carelessness. "And, anyway, how did *your* father come to have so much money, Miss Macintosh? By robbing trains out west?"

"No—by telling people where to build the tracks," Fannie said. She lifted her chin in the air defiantly, but she also looked a little scared, Hattie thought, as though she didn't know quite how she'd gotten into this particular pickle.

"I should have known!" Sophie said—which didn't make any sense at all, not in Hattie's opinion. But Sophie marched from the dining room without a backward glance, as though she'd won her point.

Mollie ducked her head and followed her.

Julie looked at Hattie questioningly, then at Fannie. "Excuse me," she said in her most polite voice, and she got to her feet.

Hattie gripped the seat of her chair, trying to decide whether or not to make it unanimous and follow the rest of the Quartette from the dining room.

"We ought to go, too," Lulu said. "I'm still supposed to rest with my limbs elevated, the doctor says," she added, blushing a little.

She, Lydia, and Daisy left the room. Only Hattie and Carrie were left.

"Well, they pulled foot fast enough," Fannie drawled, seemingly unconcerned. She turned to Hattie and Carrie. "Don't you two *ladies* have somewhere to go?" she asked, one corner of her mouth quirking up in a strained smile.

"I do," Carrie said. "I really mean it, though. I have to rewrite that stupid essay on Mr. Ralph Waldo Emerson. If I don't finish it on time, Miss Brownback says she's going to make me copy it out backward."

"You'd better go, then," Fannie said, a real smile appearing on her face for the first time that afternoon.

Carrie hesitated, her wide face pink with emotion. "Thank you, though, Fannie—for everything. This has been the best Sunday ever," she said. "It's about time someone stood up to that Minnie Bonesteel!" She hurried from the room.

"Huh," Fannie said, and then she turned to Hattie. "So, what are you still doing here?" she asked coolly.

"I don't know," Hattie said, speaking the simple truth.

"Don't you care about your reputation?" Fannie asked.

She looked down and twisted her napkin around her finger as she spoke.

"Yes," Hattie admitted slowly, "I *have* to care. Why, I barely even have a reputation. You know that. And if I *do* have one, it's because Sophie's father bought it for me," she added, surprised that she could be so candid with Fannie. "He's in business, too," she added, a little defiantly.

Fannie looked uncomfortable. "I didn't mean to hurt Sophie's feelings," she said, looking up. "Sometimes I just get carried away." Suddenly, she gave Hattie a piercing look. "You hurt *my* feelings when you wouldn't talk to me, but I think maybe we're two of a kind."

Like seeks like. Minnie Bonesteel's old jeer seemed to echo in Hattie's head. "No!" Hattie protested, jumping to her feet. "I'm nowhere *near* as bold as you," she added, trying to soften her protest.

Fannie laughed, but it didn't seem as though she thought anything really very funny was going on. "Don't get all huffed. Believe it or not, I didn't mean it as an insult," she said. "I only meant you're not a snob like Minnie Bonesteel or—or your cousin Sophie, though I'm sorry to say it of her. And you and I are all alone in the world, or just about."

"I had a little brother, once." Hattie was amazed to hear the words leave her mouth. It was the first time she'd mentioned Joey to anyone, even to Sophie, since that time in July. She sat down again with a *thud.*

"What was his name?"

"Jotham." Hattie practically breathed the word. "We called him Joey. He died just last winter. In January."

"How old?"

"Only five. The influenza. Sometimes—sometimes I think that God isn't worth shucks."

"God *isn't* worth shucks," Fannie confirmed. "He lets all sorts of bad things happen, don't he?"

Hattie nodded, glum.

"What was Joey like?" Fannie asked softly.

Hattie sighed, remembering. "He found a baby squirrel once. I guess it had fallen out of its nest or something, but Joey decided that he was going to be its papa. It was an awful thing, all wrinkly. Its eyes were squinched shut, its ears were all pasted down, and it had a face like a little pink raisin. But Joey loved it hard, he did. Wrapped it in a flannel and soaked a little rag in milk to make a teat for the squirrel to suck on. I helped," Hattie added.

"But it died, I'll bet," Fannie said. "They always do."

Hattie nodded. She couldn't bring herself to mention Joey's heartbroken sobs or the little burial she and her brother had secretly performed, knowing Aunt Lydia would never approve of such a heathenish thing—glorifying a *rodent*.

Hattie couldn't tell Fannie the most painful thing of all, though—that her memory of Joey was fading almost minute by minute. His hair? Blazing red. His eyes? Clear water green. His nose? Snub, with freckles. But these scrappy images were like puzzle pieces, and she could no longer put them together to form one coherent image.

"I feel so—so lonely-like, most of the time," Fannie confided suddenly. "Everything I try to say or do to make friends comes out wrong, wrong, wrong."

Hattie sighed, mute with pity.

"God isn't worth shucks," Fannie repeated, "and we *are* two of a kind."

But at these words, Hattie could remain silent no longer. First Sophie tried to put her in a box, and now Fannie was doing the same thing. "No, we're not. We're not alike, you and I! *You're* not alone—you still have a father, don't you?"

"Yes, somewhere," Fannie said, nodding. "I went everywhere with him, after Mama left us. Virginia City, like I told you about, but also Tucson, even San Francisco and, oh, lots of places. Then we'd come back to New York once a year for shopping and a frolic. But he's older than other girls' papas, see, and he started worrying about dragging me around with him all the time. 'Specially once I started to grow maguppies," she added, gazing sadly down at her chest. "He said men were starting to stare at me, so he sent me away." Her dark eyes glistened, and she gazed at her napkin for a moment. "Look," she said, finally glancing up, "I'm sorry that it made you sad, talking about Joey that way."

"Please don't say his name," Hattie said, her voice fierce. She was sorry she'd even mentioned him to Fannie, and she almost hated Fannie for making her do it.

Fannie held up her nail-bitten hand in a gesture of

surrender. "It's just that I'm something of a border ruffian, that's all," she said, "and you—well, you're a poor relation, to hear some folks talk. And an orphan, to boot. I guess I just meant that we're both on the outside, a little bit."

"I'm not on the outside," Hattie protested. "I'm Sophie Hubbard's cousin."

"I thought there was more to you than that," Fannie said after a moment. "I thought you had a special outsidey kind of way of looking at the world—as I do."

"Well, you're wrong about that," Hattie said in a shaky voice. "I'm not outsidey at all! I'm just like the others—and happy to be so. Why, I'm part of the Quartette, or haven't you heard?"

Fannie didn't answer this question. Finally though, after a moment, she said, "I reckon I made a mistake about you, then. You'd better go. I suppose I would, if I had such friends waiting for me."

And so Hattie left the dining room, too.

17

WINDOW

Yesterday afternoon we went for a walk over the hill and got caught in the rain and had to run home. We were heated and had to cool off, which we did by parading through Mol's room with our drawers rolled up, all superfluous clothing being discarded. Miss Brownback walked in, in the midst of our fun.

I would like to know what she thinks of us . . .

"What *does* Miss Brownback think of us, I wonder?" Hattie asked Julie, closing her journal, which she'd been reading to herself. The girls in the Quartette were taking turns brushing one another's hair.

Julie thought for a moment, wooden hairbrush in hand. Her flowered robe sagged open, revealing a flannel night-gown of blue-and-green tartan. Heavy gray woolen socks warmed her feet. "I suspect she thinks that we're silly and spoiled," she finally said, and recommenced brushing Hattie's dark brown hair.

"*I'm* not spoiled," Mollie scoffed. Her three friends looked at her and then burst into laughter. Mollie was wrapped in a bottle green cashmere robe, with the lavish frills of a pale green kitten-soft nightgown peeking out from beneath the hem. Shearling slippers kept her feet warm. "I'm not spoiled!" Mollie objected.

"Oh, come on, Mol—with all the fine dresses your mother sends you?" Sophie said. "Why, I think her seamstress must just about live with your dress form. It probably seems to her as if she has another daughter! And what about those hampers of treats your mother sends from Bridgeport each week?"

"Not that we're complaining," Julie said hastily. She lifted a sugar-encrusted cookie from a tin that balanced on Sophie's neatly folded rose-and-cream quilt and took an appreciative bite. "Mmm," she said. "You have the best cook, Mol. Thanksgiving is going to be wonderful this year. I can't believe we'll be leaving tomorrow."

"*I* can't believe we'll all be together for the holiday," Hattie said, pulling her thick red woolen socks up as high as they'd go, then tugging the pleated flannel sleeves of her own wrap over her hands to keep them warm.

She was glad they were all going to be together, she told herself—after all, if she was going to show herself to the world as one of the Quartette, why, that's where her loyalties should lie.

"I've never been to Bridgeport before," Sophie said excitedly, combing a snarl out of Mollie's curly hair with care. "What's it like?"

"You'll see soon enough," Mollie said, her voice still a little frosty. She brooded for a moment, then blurted out, "It's not as though you girls aren't spoiled, too. All except for Hattie, I mean. She doesn't count."

I don't count, Hattie thought, momentarily shaken.

"Oh, Mol," Sophie said, shaking her head.

"I'm sorry, Hattie," Mollie said, instantly contrite. "I was trying to say a *good* thing—that you aren't spoiled."

"It's all right," Hattie murmured.

"Will we meet Mr. Barnum?" Julie said, to change the course of this discussion. Phineas Taylor Barnum—known as P. T. Barnum—was the founder and owner of the most famous circus in the entire world.

"We're bound to," Mollie said. "He lives in Seaside Park, too, just down the road a bit. He's quite an old gentleman, now, but he'll be around. The entire circus is in Bridgeport during the winter. Mr. Barnum even has his gardener use a camel and a zebra to pull the mower when it's time to cut the lawns. You should see the look on the gardener's face! He hates making such a spectacle of himself, but Mr. B insists."

Hattie giggled, trying to imagine it. She *did* feel as though she were a real part of the Quartette, she reassured herself—in spite of Mollie's thoughtless comment.

"Why, you never know what you'll see next in Bridge-port," Mollie continued. "You might even meet General Tom Thumb strolling down the road while you're in town."

"I'll try not to step on him," Julie said.

"Oh, he's not *that* small," Mollie said earnestly, and as usual, missing her friend's irony. "He's quite dapper, really."

"Then I'll try not to fall in love with him," Julie said.

"He's already married," Mollie said, shaking her head.

"Fall in love," Sophie mused aloud. "I'll wager *that's* what Miss Brownback thinks—that we're not concentrating on French dialogue or rhetoric or mathematics at all while we're here, we're simply waiting to fall in love in a few more years."

"I don't know," Julie objected. "We're awfully young to be thinking about that."

"Not according to Miss Macintosh," Sophie snapped.

Mollie and Julie looked at Hattie at the mention of Fannie's name, but Hattie looked unconcerned—despite the pounding in her chest. It had been a full week since she and Fannie had spoken in the dining room. Fannie had resumed her silent ways since that last talk, seeming almost to sleep-walk, now, through her days at Miss Bulkley's. It was making everyone uncomfortable—especially Hattie.

I can't do anything about it, though, she reassured her-self. *It's not my responsibility.*

"I'm never getting married," Julie announced suddenly.

"Of course you are," Mollie scoffed. "You're a pretty

girl, Jules, as you very well know."

"Being pretty has nothing to do with whether a girl gets married or not," Julie said, blushing a little.

"But what *are* you going to do if you don't marry?" Sophie asked her. "Teach school like Miss Brownback and Miss Patton?"

"Maybe. Or perhaps I'll be a nurse."

Sophie laughed, pounding her fist upon her quilt. "You couldn't even take my splinter out the other day! You had to put your head down to keep from fainting, or don't you remember?"

"Jules is fragile," Mollie announced romantically, taking her friend's defense. "Just like Anne, in Miss Woolson's book."

The four girls were silent for a moment, in honor of their current heroine.

"I'm sorry to disappoint you," Julie finally said thoughtfully, "but I'm about as fragile as a horse."

Mollie shuddered. "I'll try to forget you ever said that."

Hattie looked around the room. Everyone was quiet and still. Why, it was as though they were caught in time for the moment, like that poor little fly suspended in amber she had seen once at a traveling display of natural artifacts.

"What's the matter, Hattie?" Julie asked, concerned by the serious look on Hattie's face.

"Nothing," Hattie replied. "I was thinking, that's all."

"Well, no time for nonsense like *thinking* at Miss Bulkley's

Seminary," Julie said briskly. "It's your turn, now."

And she handed Hattie the hairbrush.

The next morning, Monday, the Quartette departed for Bridgeport for the Thanksgiving holidays. As Hattie was about to enter Mr. Purdy's hack, the last of the four girls to climb in, something made her look back at the house for a moment.

Silhouetted in one of the belvedere windows was Fannie Macintosh, watching them leave. Fannie started to duck behind her gauzy curtain, but then she paused.

I should wave good-bye, Hattie thought dully, but it was as though the window that separated her from Fannie had pinned her down, immobilizing her.

Fannie wasn't waving either.

"Hattie, come *on*," an impatient voice from within the carriage called.

And so Hattie turned her back on Fannie, the window, and the house, and clambered into the carriage. "Gee-*up!*" Mr. Purdy shouted, and the hack swayed off down Broadway, heading for the depot.

18

MEET MR. P. T. BARNUM!

I *have seen Bridgeport. Oh! Bridgeport is as perfect as a place can be. I am worn out with my longings and must retire to dream of—* Bridgeport!

Hattie Knowlton had never had so much fun in her life, those first few days of her stay in Seaside Park. Thoughts of Fannie occasionally darkened the brightness, much as a cloud's shadow might float over even the most perfect picnic lunch, but Hattie simply waited, and the thoughts faded away.

She had chosen who she was to associate with, she thought—so why not enjoy life?

And Fannie was surely all right, Hattie told herself. Why, she was probably enjoying the holiday in Manhattan with her pa's fancy friend that very moment. Lucky Fannie!

She'd come back to Miss Bulkley's much refreshed, and with new finery to wear.

Mollie's family knew everyone in Bridgeport, Connecticut, it seemed, and so the Quartette was issued many invitations. Two afternoon tea parties were given, each hosted by one of Mollie's childhood friends, although there were guests of all ages at both parties.

The liveliest of the tea parties started out quietly enough, but it ended with charades so riotous that Sophie suffered a bad case of the hiccups, much to her embarrassment, when she got carried away and rather daringly tried to act out the title of the old song, "You Naughty, Naughty Men."

Mollie and her parents hosted their own traditional gala, an open house for their neighbors, two nights before Thanksgiving. The Quartette took special care over their appearances at this event.

Mrs. Brainerd had surprised Mollie with a new gown, fitted close and made from blue satin that matched the color of her eyes. With pearls at her throat, tiny Mollie looked like a porcelain shepherdess, Hattie thought.

Slender Julie's hair was curly enough to suit even her, for once. Mrs. Brainerd's own maid had helped her to style it for the party, pulling it back into a loose knot and then freeing enough tendrils with an orangewood stick so that Julie's angular face looked softer, somehow. Dressed in rich brown with cream-colored lace at her neck, Julie had never looked prettier.

Sophie was radiant. Aunt Margaret had sent a gown to Bridgeport especially for the party. Madame Honfleur had outdone herself; Sophie's gown was an elegant mustard color, which enhanced her fairness to the extent that she seemed almost to glow from within.

Hattie wore her own best gown, naturally, the one fitted just the summer before. Its dark green velvet bodice curved prettily, she admitted privately to herself, and the white ruffle of her under-blouse framed her features in a most becoming way.

As they complimented each other on their dresses, Hattie wondered what Fannie would have worn—what outrageous outfit she might have concocted. But she squelched the thought quickly.

"Here, Hattie, I want you to wear these tonight," Mollie said, moments before they went downstairs to greet the arriving guests. She clasped a string of gold beads around Hattie's neck. Sophie and Julie nodded their approval.

Hattie stared at herself in Mollie's long mirror. She wouldn't look at all like the youngest girl at the party, she reassured herself; even less did she look like anyone's poor relation.

She *did* belong.

The Quartette huddled in the middle of Mollie's bedroom and clasped hands that were cold with excitement. Their faces were so close together that Hattie could smell cinnamon on someone's breath.

They looked solemnly and searchingly at each other. "Let us never forget this moment," Sophie said in her most portentous voice.

"Let us always remember that we are great beauties, just like the Empress Eugénie," Mollie said, almost breathless with excitement.

"Let us be glad we have one another," Hattie contributed.

"Let us hope we don't fall down the stairs," Julie intoned, eyes closed.

Fir green, sky blue, acorn brown, and leaf gold: the Quartette was the very picture of a brilliant late-autumn day as they descended the Brainerds' broad staircase, arms linked and little bustles swaying.

And for Hattie, at that moment, there was not a cloud in the sky.

Each of the big room's four silvery chandeliers held sixteen honey-colored candles, and their flickering light cast a magical glow. A few people had already gathered in front of a crackling fire; the fireplace was framed by green and white marble squares set in a checkerboard pattern Hattie greatly admired.

That geometric design was echoed in the room's ceiling, which was composed of another series of squares. Each contained a hand-painted quatrefoil design, dull gold on red, and each was surrounded by carved dark wooden beams.

Red-patterned walls were almost obscured by the landscape paintings hung upon them, framed heavily in gold: dark trees, cloudy skies, shadowed fields, and often, Hattie noticed, a little red-figured man in the painting's lower left corner.

Built-in bookcases topped with carved wooden swags lined the entire fireplace wall. The jewel-colored leather bindings made the books within these glass-fronted cases seem full of promise to Hattie, as was the evening itself. This was her chance to shine—to show the world that she deserved to move in distinguished circles, just as Sophie, Mollie, and Julie did.

As the night wore on, however, and more and more guests filled the spacious room, the party's magic faded for Hattie. Clearly, Mrs. Brainerd did not consider being a hostess an easy or enjoyable task, and she seemed determined to share this carefully disguised attitude with as many underlings as possible.

All too soon, Mollie was anxiously responding to fierce glances from her formidable mother. A reluctant Sophie assisted Mollie in her assigned tasks, both girls scurrying to carry out Mrs. Brainerd's orders—to make an introduction here, *darling*; or talk to the silent newcomer over there, *lambie*. Mrs. Brainerd attempted to soften each command with an endearment.

Mollie's little face, usually so vivid with fun and feeling, began looking pinched and anxious. Sophie merely looked bored.

Julie was standing by the bookshelf wall, chattering over animatedly to some people the girls had met earlier in their visit. Even this spirited girl felt ill at ease at such a party, Hattie reflected gloomily.

Hattie's own place of refuge was in the corner, behind a curved-back velvet chair that matched the color of her bodice. She felt almost invisible behind that chair.

Nearby stood Mr. Brainerd's big globe of the world. Hattie twirled the globe thoughtfully, toyed with one of the chair's ropey silk tassels, and generally tried to look both occupied and happy, all alone.

Oh, she thought mournfully, how can it be that the party a person looks forward to the most can turn out to be the most nerve-racking?

Hattie turned the globe again, more gently this time. Watching people at parties might be like reading palms—Gypsy-style—to tell the future, she thought suddenly, staring as entire continents seemed to float by, yellow, pink, green . . .

Perhaps she could imagine her friends' futures simply by watching their party performances, she mused. Maybe Julie would always feel a little uneasy around others, for instance, so smart and sharpish was she.

Mollie would probably always scurry through life—but prettily!—so as to carry out first her mother's wishes, Hattie thought, and then her husband's. Mollie would do what was expected of her; in the end, all that spoiling had served to make her obedient.

And as for Sophie—well, her domineering cousin would always manage to get her own way, Hattie suspected. But that way most likely would be very much like Aunt Margaret's.

Hattie did not excuse herself from her own harsh inspection. Could she imagine her own future judged by her party behavior, too? Based upon her performance so far, she hoped not. She was removed, isolated, alone . . . watching the party but not really part of it. Was this to be her fate?

It didn't have to be—not according to Fannie. One's fate should be a choice, as far as was possible, not an assignment, something you were pushed into.

Fannie had taught her that, she realized.

Hattie turned again to watch Mollie, who was biting her lips and exchanging furtive glances with an increasingly impatient Sophie as Mrs. Brainerd leaned forward, her face creased with displeasure over some small transgression.

Fannie Macintosh would never abide being terrorized by such a one, Hattie thought, suddenly outraged. Not for a minute! She'd be having *fun* on a night like this. Why, if you can't have fun at a party, when can you?

But how much fun was she, Hattie, having?

And then, Hattie simply dared herself.

She took a deep breath and walked over to the liveliest group of people at the party. They were standing by the fireplace, small berry-colored glasses glittering in their hands.

"How do," Hattie said shyly, after striding right up to

the jolliest-looking old man in the crowd. She bobbed a curtsy.

This was, she thought dizzily, the Fannie Macintosh thing to do.

"Well, *hello*," the man said, much amused, and he stuck out a big hand for Hattie to shake. His long snowy side-whiskers stood out in sharp contrast against the red of his cheeks. He looked as though he had been gently inflated in some mysterious way; it seemed he might pop if a person poked him too hard.

Hattie shook his hand gingerly and curtsied again.

Mrs. Brainerd and Mollie appeared at Hattie's side as if summoned by a wizard; Mollie's mother seemed taken aback at Hattie's boldness. "Harriet, meet Mr. P. T. Barnum! Taylor, this is Miss Harriet Knowlton," she said, making the introductions.

"Harriet is also called Hattie, Mr. B," Mollie contributed, relaxing a little. She was clearly a great favorite of Mr. Barnum's.

Hattie felt almost breathless; her daring was fading fast. Why, Mr. Barnum was famous all over the *world* for his circus!

"This girl has two names?" Mr. Barnum said, pretending to be puzzled. "Just exactly how old *are* you, my dear?"

"I'm almost fifteen, sir," Hattie told him in a voice she barely recognized as her own, so confident did it sound.

"Why, that means you have one name for every seven

years you've been on this earth." His tone was solemn, but his eyes were bright with merriment. "Thank heavens you're not any older than that, Miss Hattie," he joked, "or else who *knows* how many names I'd have to remember? My aged brain can only hold so much." He tapped at his head three times, and his tongue clacked against his teeth when he did so, as if his head was empty—and echoing.

Everyone laughed.

"She'll only be here for a few days," Mrs. Brainerd told him. "You needn't trouble yourself." Mrs. Brainerd was trying to speak in a jocular tone to match Mr. Barnum's, but Hattie could tell that Mollie's mother didn't like all the attention she was getting from their esteemed neighbor.

Mr. Barnum wouldn't be hurried, though. "Hattie!" he said to his small audience, rocking back on his heels in front of the fire blazing in the big fireplace. "In my day, I don't mind telling you that young ladies didn't have such sprightly names—oh, no."

"What were they called then, Mr. B?" Mollie asked eagerly.

"Oh, they had sober and sensible names, like Asenath or Hester or Thankful. Why, I even knew a girl named Submit, when I was a boy," he said, beaming as proudly as if he had just performed a conjuring trick.

"*Submit!*" Mollie whispered, pleasantly horrified.

"And very nice names those were, too," Mrs. Brainerd said stoutly. She didn't like the idea of nicknames at all, not one little bit. No Mol, Soph, Jules, or Hattie around *her*, thank you very much.

"Mother, those old-timey names were simply *awful*," Mollie insisted bravely. Mrs. Brainerd hid her answering scowl; there were too many people around to reply to her daughter as she might have wished.

"Well, those names are nothing like as distinguished as *Hattie*," Mr. Barnum said gallantly.

"Thank you, sir," Hattie said, sounding quite at ease. She would tell Fannie all about this little triumph, she vowed on the spot—just as soon as she got back to school.

She was done with following Sophie's wishes. She would determine her own fate. And part of that fate meant becoming friends—real friends—with Fannie Macintosh, by gosh!

As for Sophie . . . well, Sophie would simply have to bear it, that was all, Hattie decided. Surely her headstrong cousin was capable of withstanding a *little* insurrection.

"Have you been to see my circus?" Mr. Barnum asked Hattie.

"Oh, Taylor," Mrs. Brainerd whispered, but so that everyone could hear. "I hardly think Miss Harriet's purse could ever run to *that*. She's an orphan, Mollie tells me—she hasn't a bean. The Hubbards took her in out of charity, bless their hearts."

Behind Hattie, Sophie gasped.

"Mother!" Mollie cried.

Hattie stood still, the smile frozen on her face as the

group of people around her murmured sympathetically. Suddenly, the gown she loved felt like a costume, and as for the gold beads Mollie had lent her, Hattie wanted to rip them from her neck and fling them into the fireplace.

"We all need a helping hand now and again," Mr. Barnum said, as if unaware of the impact this news was making. "Nothing wrong with charity."

Hearing these words, Hattie realized what Fannie already knew, and had tried to tell her, and what she, Hattie, should already have known: that there *was* no shame in being poor and needing a hand. The shame belonged to those who thought poverty was an embarrassment, a humiliation, something to be whispered and gossiped about.

"No, there's nothing wrong with charity," Hattie said firmly. "Why, it's charity that enables us to forgive." She gave Mrs. Brainerd a cool, appraising look, then excused herself and left the party.

19

THANKSGIVING

*O*ne of the newly arrived elephants at the winter quarters is being trained to answer to the name of 'Hattie,' by special order of Mr. Barnum. This is done in honor of a young lady of Tarrytown, who is visiting here and who is known by that peculiar soubriquet."

Mr. Brainerd finished reading the newspaper article aloud. He gave a quick bark of laughter and then handed the newspaper to Mollie, seated next to him, gesturing that it was to be passed around the laden Thanksgiving table. Mollie had been busy attempting to pick the oysters from her helping of dressing, but she stopped long enough to read the words for herself.

"It's a triumph, my dear," Mr. Brainerd told Hattie.

"Yes," Mollie said, looking up from the article. Her

pleading smile seemed to ask, *Doesn't this make everything better?*

Across the table, Hattie smiled wanly and speared a pickle with a little fork. Her head felt hot—perhaps from the overheated room, she thought, or the tiny slosh of champagne Mr. Brainerd's butler had poured for each of the girls.

"Oh, Horace—don't exaggerate so," Mrs. Brainerd said crankily from the opposite end of the table. She gestured for the mashed potatoes to be passed once more and helped herself first.

"Be careful, my dear, or Taylor will name an elephant for *you*," Mr. Brainerd joked, looking at his wife's crowded plate.

Mollie tried to hide her smile. "But Mr. Barnum did it to honor Hattie, don't forget," she told her father. "He said it was because she was such a little sweetheart." She looked at Hattie beseechingly. *Forgive us*, her eyes seemed to say.

"Her name is Harriet, dear, not Hattie," her mother said, swallowing hard.

"All right—he called the elephant 'Hattie' to honor Harriet," Mollie corrected herself, though her correction had made her statement lose its meaning, Hattie thought muzzily.

Her head was beginning to ache.

"Turkey, miss?" a maid asked, and a platter was nudged under Hattie's left elbow.

"No, thank you," Hattie murmured, shrinking back at the sight of the steaming slices of meat. Her stomach turned.

Was she ill? She'd felt strange since that morning, when she'd finally had it out with her friends. "Well, I'm sorry for what Mother said," she remembered Mollie saying, "but it's not *my* fault you're poor."

"Hattie's not poor," Sophie asserted hotly.

"Oh, Soph—of course I am," Hattie said. "Why is it such a crime? Why does it shame you so?"

"I don't know," Sophie said, confused.

"It's not as though any of you ever did a thing in this world to merit your wealth," Hattie said, facing her friends. "And, besides, that's not what angers me."

"What *does* anger you?" Julie asked.

"Being betrayed," Hattie said—because clearly, Mollie, at least, had been gossiping about her behind her back.

And she, Hattie, was an embarrassment to Sophie, her own cousin.

Only Fannie Macintosh would understand how it felt to be betrayed like that.

Why, of course she would, Hattie thought suddenly, blushing—for hadn't Fannie been betrayed by a friend, too?

Hadn't she, *Hattie*, betrayed her? And Fannie was the only girl she could speak the unvarnished truth to—about Joey, about her past.

Hattie took a deep breath and forced herself to raise her eyes to the Thanksgiving table, much in the spirit of looking out at the horizon in an attempt to avoid a bout of seasickness.

Heavy silver candlesticks marched down the Brainerds' long Thanksgiving table's still-snowy surface, each one's sinuous arms holding two yellow candles. The smell of beeswax mingled with turkey, oyster dressing, spiced peaches, and potatoes, sweet, au gratin, and mashed. The remains of a cauliflower head—encircled with bright green peas, and cloaked with a cheese sauce that was by now looking a little the worse for wear—faced Hattie like a foe, while giblet lumps glistened sickeningly as they bobbed in the ornate silver gravy boat that sat before her.

The remnants of a roast suckling pig with a withered apple in its mouth, preserved cherries skewered to its eyes, and a necklace of sausages around its neck, hulked just down the table.

"You should be thrilled, Hattie," Mollie said. "Why, there are only two or three elephants in this entire country! *Thousands* of folks will come to see this darling little one and wonder how she got her name."

"Don't say 'folks,' Mollie," her mother instructed. "It's vulgar."

"Hat—I mean, *Harriet* doesn't *look* thrilled," Julie observed, tilting her head as she looked across the table at her friend. "She looks rather green, in fact."

All eyes were now on Hattie, much to her horror.

"She *does* look a bit green," Sophie said. "Are you all right?

"Why, of course she's all right," Mr. Brainerd boomed.

"There's nothing wrong with Miss Harriet that a little apple pie won't cure, I'll wager. Or perhaps a slice of walnut sherry cake," he added temptingly. "What do you say to that, my dear?"

But Hattie couldn't say anything at all—she was running from the room.

"Well, I never!" Mrs. Brainerd's exasperated exclamation followed Hattie out the door.

Three long, miserable days later, poor sick Hattie wanted nothing more than to return to Tarrytown. "Don't leave me," she begged the others—only half joking—as they departed for the Bridgeport Depot.

"We have to go back. Classes start again tomorrow. But we'll miss you," Sophie promised. "Have you truly forgiven us?" she added, her blue eyes brimming with tears.

"I didn't mean to say anything to Mama about you," Mollie said, shaking her curly head. "But she kept asking and asking!"

"We're all friends again, aren't we?" Julie asked.

"Yes," Hattie said, meaning it. Now that she had spoken her mind, she realized she *was* friends with them—but on her terms, not theirs. "I only wish you weren't leaving," she repeated.

"Don't worry, Hattie," Mollie said. "My mother will take good care of you."

"Ohhh," Hattie groaned.

Julie looked sympathetic. "Pretend you're asleep whenever Mrs. Brainerd comes into the room," she whispered, and then she and Mollie left.

Sophie brushed her hand gently across Hattie's forehead. "Do you really feel better?"

"Yes—compared to how I felt Thanksgiving Day," Hattie told her. And compared to the way I felt at the Brainerds' party, she added silently.

Sophie grimaced as if she'd been able to hear Hattie's thoughts, but then suddenly she smiled. "I can't believe that you were mentioned in the newspaper, Hattie! You'll be famous at school."

"It will be fun telling Fannie," Hattie said. Sophie started to pull away, but Hattie held tight to her small warm hand, and she gave it another loving squeeze.

Sophie sighed. "Well, I suppose it *is* her kind of story," she finally conceded, and she couldn't help but smile a little.

Perched high in one of the Brainerds' turreted guest rooms, and swathed in a gray satin bed jacket belonging to Mrs. Brainerd, Hattie heard cheery scraps of laughter rise from the curved gravel drive below, then the sound of carriage wheels crunched their own good-bye.

The girls were gone. Immensely sorry for herself all of a sudden, Hattie blinked back a few hot tears.

Out the window, late November light gleamed on the dark water of the Sound. Hattie could see the north shore of

Long Island clearly from her bed, despite the steely clouds that hovered overhead.

"Bouillon, miss," a soft voice said. "I'll set up the tray for you."

"Thank you," Hattie said. The hot salty broth would feel good on her stomach, but she'd have to keep from spilling any of it on Mrs. Brainerd's silky blue blanket cover. She winced merely thinking of the possibility.

"Poor wee thing," the maid said. Her rosy face twisted in sympathy. "Do you need the basin, then?"

"No, thank you," Hattie said, cheering up at once. She almost laughed at being called *wee*. Wee, when she always felt so clumsy next to tiny Mol! Hattie picked up a heavy soup spoon and tried not to clink it—giantess-style—against the delicate soup plate.

"That's better," the maid said, pleased.

Hattie dozed after her lunch, her pleasant Sunday afternoon drowsiness only half spoiled by the thought of impending visits from the dreaded Mrs. Brainerd or the family doctor, who looked in on her each day.

Oh, it was awful being sick in someone else's house, Hattie thought. She vowed to stay well forevermore.

Hattie tried to picture Sophie and Julie and Mollie—who would be in the train by now—racing along the Connecticut shore toward the city, where they would change trains for Tarrytown, clutching their reticules against pickpockets. Soph and Mol might be chattering away, reliving the various excitements of their holiday. Jules would be reading. What fun they were probably having!

Hattie reached for her journal and opened it to her favorite page. *"One of the newly arrived elephants at the winter quarters is being trained to answer to the name of 'Hattie,' by special order of Mr. Barnum . . ."*

Could anything more exciting have happened to any girl at Miss Bulkley's over the Thanksgiving holiday?

If Gladys dropped a tray at the very mention of the word *elephant*, how might she respond to this thrilling news? Hattie could hardly wait to tell her.

Most of all, though, Hattie could scarcely wait to tell Fannie about the whole amazing experience of visiting the circus yard the day after the Brainerds' party, at Mr. Barnum's insistence—and especially of meeting the lumbering little creature. Her huge ragged ears had moved like creaky gray fans; her shy-seeming blink and side-stepping shuffle gave the baby elephant every appearance of not quite knowing *what* to do next; the wetness and hairiness of the nose holes at the end of her long snakey snout sucked noisily against Hattie's palm as she had held out a quivering peanut.

I'm sorry, Fannie, Hattie wanted to say. I'm sorry that up until now, I didn't have the courage to be a better friend to you.

Well, she *would* say it, just as soon as she got back to school.

Hattie downed her afternoon cup of hot chocolate with a gusto that had been absent since Thanksgiving dinner.

Two days later, still full from the food in the lunch hamper Mrs. Brainerd's cook had assembled—two turkey salad sandwiches; a packet of trimmed celery, carrots, and radishes; a hard-cooked egg with a twist of salt; three tart and crunchy Northern Spy apples; a wedge of dark chocolate cake wrapped in greaseproof paper as carefully as a Christmas present—Hattie bounced her heavy carpetbag up the front steps to Miss Bulkley's Seminary.

She felt—why, she felt as though she had come home! Hadn't Mr. Barnum said it himself? *A young lady of Tarrytown . . .*

Home. "Imagine," Hattie whispered.

Home was where her friends were—Sophie, Julie, Mollie—and Fannie Macintosh, too.

Hattie lifted the brass knocker, but before she could even let it fall, the door flew open. "It *is* you. Mrs. Halloran said she thought she heard the hack," Fiona greeted her. The girl looked troubled. Tears glinted in her thick black lashes.

Hattie dropped her bag with a thud and grabbed Fiona's arm. "What is it?" she asked, her heart pounding. "What's happened, Fee? Is it Sophie? Mol?"

"No, it's Miss Macintosh," Fiona wailed. "She's runned away, she has! And it's all because of what you wrote, Miss Harriet. Oh, how could you?"

≈ 20 ≈

S E R I O U S

arriet, how *could* you?" Miss Bulkley moaned, unknowingly repeating Fiona's plaintive words. She clasped an embroidered Chinese sofa pillow to her bosom and rocked back and forth.

Hattie looked around Miss Bulkley's private sitting room, an inner sanctum on the first floor to which no girl in known communal memory had ever been admitted before now.

The room seemed stuffed beyond understanding with framed letters, figurines, and other assorted knickknacks, gifts from the families of former students. Each item was scrupulously dusted, and all were displayed against a dark, ornately patterned wine-colored wall covering. Polished horse brasses twinkled up and down either side of Miss Bulkley's small black fireplace, which was flanked by Miss Brownback and Miss Patton, wearing matching expressions of solemnity.

The situation must be serious, Hattie thought—it must be *terrible*. "But I—I didn't do anything wrong," she repeated.

"What about this?" Miss Brownback asked quietly. She handed Hattie a crumpled piece of paper. Black ink looped, curled, and whirled with seeming abandon across its blue-lined surface.

Hattie read:

> *There is a new girl coming, a naughty, bad, wicked wild girl. She is to be tamed. I think we will manage to have fun in spite of her.*
>
> *She has come, she of the wild, ungovernable will. Our wildest conjectures have failed and she exceeds all that we feared or dared to imagine. Her name is Fannie Macintosh, by gosh, and language fails when you wish to describe her.*
>
> *I hate her! I wish she had never come to our school, and that's the truth.*
>
> *Hattie Knowlton*

Hattie looked up, her face pale. "But—but that's *not* the truth," she whispered. "Not the last part. I never said that. Why, it's not even my handwriting! And I had my journal with me in Bridgeport, so how—"

Miss Bulkley arose from her chair with surprising agility. She bounded across the room and snatched the paper from Hattie's hand. "Do—you—*deny?*" she asked, her voice choked with rage and her face suffused with unhealthy color.

Hattie couldn't catch her breath for a moment. "They were only words that I scribbled in my journal," she protested. "My *private* journal. I never showed them to anyone."

Except to Sophie, she thought suddenly.

Sophie.

But . . . how? And *why*?

Miss Brownback seemed to glide across the room, and she tugged the paper from Miss Bulkley's trembling grasp. "Why, I believe Hattie *did* just make a denial, Miss Bulkley," she said. "And this is not her handwriting, now that I have time to think about it calmly. So let's hear her out."

Miss Bulkley did not seem to hear Miss Brownback's words. She was almost gasping by then, but her eyes never moved from Hattie's face. "You—you *dare*? After I took you in at the very last minute—when there's a *waiting list* of girls wanting to attend my school?" She seemed to spit out the words.

Miss Patton tugged Miss Bulkley back to her chair and handed her the Chinese cushion as if it were a medical potion. "Take a deep breath," she commanded. "You look as if you're about to have a conniption fit."

Miss Bulkley swallowed a mouthful of air like a big fish drowning on a Hudson River dock.

Miss Brownback scrutinized the paper she was holding, and Miss Pat joined her. Miss Brownback looked up. "Well, did you *compose* this, Hattie?" she asked.

"Most of it," Hattie admitted, miserable.

They were the very words she'd taken so much pleasure in writing—and yet they had now taken on a malignant life of their own.

"What part *didn't* you compose?" Miss Patton asked.

"The part where it says that I hate Fannie, and that I wish she had never come to this school."

"But you confess to writing the rest of it?" Miss Brownback asked, rattling the paper slightly.

"Yes," Hattie said. "But—but not that way, Miss Brownback. Not exactly. Someone ran my words together! And I never meant for anyone else to see them," she added. "I wrote those words before I even *knew* Fannie."

Miss Brownback's eyes seemed to cloud with disappointment as she gazed steadily at Hattie. "She didn't know that when she read them, dear," the teacher said, shaking her sleek head sadly. She scanned the words on the paper once more, frowning thoughtfully. "First, it says that a new girl is coming, and the next thing you know, she's already here."

Hattie leaned over the paper once more. "That's because I wrote those things at different times. On different days, even. Where did you find that paper?"

"On Fannie's cot, Sunday morning," Miss Brownback said. "It was pinned to her blanket."

"Ruined," Miss Bulkley croaked. "Ruined, by a green girl from absolutely nowhere."

Is she talking about me or Fannie? Hattie wondered, numb.

Miss Brownback examined the paper more closely. "Just look at all those flourishes," she murmured. "Now, who among our girls writes like that?"

"Just about all of them," Miss Patton said, rolling her eyes with exasperation at the thought of her students' ornate handwriting. "*Someone* wrote it," she continued logically, "and someone—namely Fannie Macintosh—read it, too, and that's why she skedaddled."

"Because she thought that's the way I felt about her?" Hattie whispered.

Miss Patton nodded. "Well, you have to consider," she explained reasonably, "Fannie was all alone here in Tarrytown, wasn't she? No family, and—let's face the facts— she was as out of place as a flea at a tea party. I mean to say! Miss Brownback and I did what we could, but the only thing that really kept her going was the possibility of being friends with you one day, dear. Why, she as much as said so herself."

Hattie tried to imagine how *she* might feel as a new student at Miss Bulkley's Seminary—without the Quartette embracing her at every turn. "She *said* that?"

Miss Patton nodded again. "'Two peas in the wrong pod,' that's how she put it. But then, to cap the climax," she continued as though she were witnessing the event as it happened, "Fannie reads your words—just when she's at her lowest ebb, too, I'll wager. It doesn't take a Philadelphia lawyer to figure out what happened next."

No, it doesn't, Hattie agreed silently. "When did she leave?" she asked aloud.

"Late Saturday night, we assume," Miss Bulkley boomed, accusation still ringing in her voice. "She left most of her clothes, too, and *all* her books."

"We've simply scoured the town," Miss Patton exclaimed. "We interrogated Mr. Purdy until he practically howled, and we've haunted the depot. How could she disappear off the face of the earth this way? And if she *did* leave town, how could she get so far, so fast?"

Miss Brownback shook her head. "She could have fled to the depot on foot and slipped onto a train before we even knew she was gone. And once she got as far as the city . . ." Her voice trailed away.

"Gone," Miss Bulkley said, making a gesture of utter hopelessness with her wide white hands.

"And Fannie had money," Miss Brownback asserted. "Why, her father sent her enough to last out the year, and that was only last week. I was with her when she opened the envelope." Miss Brownback's eyes widened at the memory.

Miss Bulkley let the pillow drop to the floor. "Maybe she went shopping," she said, hope sounding in her voice. "Perhaps Miss Macintosh is simply off on a spree!"

Miss Brownback and Miss Patton looked at her, pity in their eyes.

"Ohhh," Miss Bulkley moaned.

"Miss Macintosh seemed all right on Thanksgiving,"

Miss Brownback finally said. "Subdued, but we still managed to have some fun, didn't we, Pat?"

From the other side of the fireplace, Miss Patton nodded vigorously; her braided loops of hair jiggled. "Lots of walks and reading aloud."

"But—but why did she stay *here* during the holiday?" Hattie asked.

"She didn't have anywhere else to go," Miss Brownback explained simply. "There were no relatives who could take her, and her father couldn't make it back."

"But I thought her father had a friend in the city who might—"

"Her pa will be on his way here just as soon as he can," Miss Patton interrupted grimly, "and I'll bet he'll be as mad as a hornet, too."

"Ohhh," Miss Bulkley groaned again. She held perfectly still and squinted her eyes as if envisioning a fearsome Mr. Macintosh's arrival at her school, six-shooters blazing.

"Do you know who might have shown this to Fannie?" Miss Brownback asked, turning back to Hattie.

Hattie looked at it and thought for a moment. She knew who must have copied out her journal entry in the first place: Sophie.

It did look a *little* like Sophie's handwriting. Some of it, anyway. But Fannie left the note on her own pillow Saturday night, Hattie thought, and Sophie hadn't returned to school until Sunday.

Sophie might well have shown those words to Mol and Jules, though—in fact, she probably *had* shown them Hattie's words, in spite of Hattie having told her that long-ago October night that she didn't want to read her journal aloud to the others.

But Sophie would never have let Fannie see what Hattie had written—and she certainly wouldn't have added those hateful final words.

Would she?

Thoughts whirling, Hattie shook her head in mute reply to Miss Brownback's question, then refolded the paper and stealthily slipped it into her coat pocket as the Misses Brownback and Patton tried anew to console a shuddering Miss Bulkley.

No, I don't know for sure who showed this to Fannie—but I'll find out, Hattie thought savagely.

Gladys poked her red head into the fusty room and bobbed an awkward curtsy. "Dominie Spencer's here," she announced, sounding scared. "Oh, and Mrs. Spencer, too."

THAT POOR CHILD

*D*ominie Spencer strode through the door, his wife trailing behind him. "I came as soon as I could," he announced grandly, letting his cape drop to the floor. He looked like an overstuffed opera singer making an onstage entrance, Hattie couldn't help but think.

Mrs. Spencer leaned over to pick up the cape in spite of her own burden, a swaddled bundle that must be her newest baby, Hattie realized. Boy number eight. "I'll get that," Hattie told Mrs. Spencer, and she handed the Dominie's plush wrap to Gladys, who was making tender clucking sounds and trying to get a peek at the infant.

"Well, thank you for coming, Dominie," Miss Bulkley said. She gestured graciously with one hand for him to sit, and with the other for Gladys to stop her gawping *instantly*— Hattie could almost hear the words in her ferocious look— and get them all some tea, for heaven's sake.

Miss Brownback and Miss Patton exchanged glances. "Please sit down, Mrs. Spencer," Miss Patton said, offering the woman a chair. Mrs. Spencer gratefully sank into it.

"How perfectly sweet. What a lamb," Miss Brownback said, leaning over the baby, whose creased red face immediately grimaced. He batted at himself with tiny clenched fists and spat up a little curd of milk.

"His name is Algernon," Mrs. Spencer said, pleased at the attention in spite of the circumstances.

"Mrs. Spencer insisted on accompanying me," Dominie Spencer said, eyeing his wife and infant with distaste.

"I had to come," Mrs. Spencer said, leaning forward. "That poor child." Tears filled her eyes.

"We had no way of knowing," Miss Bulkley said, somewhat vaguely.

Miss Bulkley was going to have to do better than that when Fannie's father swept into Tarrytown, Hattie thought.

"Of course you hadn't," Dominie Spencer soothed, and Miss Bulkley gave him a look made up in equal parts of gratitude and calculation. Hattie could almost hear the woman's thought: Will this man help me when Mr. Macintosh arrives?

Hattie knew the answer to that question, too: Not a chance in the world! If the past was any indication, the Dominie would make himself scarce at the very first sign of conflict.

Gladys crashed into the sitting room carrying a tea tray.

Fee was close behind, balancing a plate filled with hastily made sandwiches. Dominie Spencer craned his neck to look at the food, and he licked his lips like a cat eyeing somebody's prized goldfish.

"Did you look for Miss Macintosh at the depot, or down around Bird Avenue?" Mrs. Spencer asked, after accepting a cup of tea from Gladys with a grateful murmur.

"Of course," Miss Bulkley said, not even looking at her.

"We did that the very first thing," Miss Brownback assured her.

"You shouldn't berate yourself, Miss Bulkley," Dominie Spencer said, although Miss Bulkley had, of course, done nothing of the kind. "Some souls were simply made to be lost," he added, spraying bread crumbs. He poked delicately at the corner of his mouth with a pudgy little finger and nodded his small head once, as if for punctuation.

Miss Patton stared at the man as though he was a particularly loathsome specimen of insect. "I don't recall reading that in *my* Bible," she observed.

Miss Bulkley bridled. "Well, I'm certain it's in there somewhere if the Dominie says it is."

"That poor child," Mrs. Spencer said again.

That poor child.

Unbidden, the memories flooded back.

Hattie recalled kneeling in the small square bedroom in Hammons Mill. It was February, a hundred years ago, it seemed, and it was so cold that she had to press the palms of her hands together to say a simple prayer, rather than interlace her fingers as she did when her aunt was watching.

Great-Aunt Lydia's friends from church—her *mourners*—were using most of the household's remaining fuel to keep little Joey warm—or to *try* to keep him warm. Nothing seemed to work, though, not since he'd fallen ill.

Hattie had greeted the doctor and then fled upstairs. Dr. Leavitt insisted on being alone when he examined Joey, but Hattie had to admit she did not want to hear her little brother cry out at the sight of the man, which might easily set him to coughing again—that terrifyingly wheezy, burbling sound she had come to dread.

Hattie could no longer bear even to hear Joey whimper when the doctor began prodding him with his thick fingers. It was as though the man felt obliged to do *something*, however useless, when he visited his little patient.

Dr. Dandy, Hattie called Dr. Leavitt secretly, and with scorn. She thought of the man's too-shiny ankle boots and the romantically swooping Inverness cape that he always handed to her without even a glance, saying, "Here, Miss Harriet."

A muffled wail floated up the stairs and slid under the door to Hattie's room; it was followed by a series of rapid, panicky coughs. She bit her lower lip as hard as she could, stifling a cry of her own.

Her hands flew up to cover her ears.

Poor little Joey, Hattie thought. Poor Aunt. Poor everyone. She rubbed her hands hard against her eyes, until sparks of light seemed to form little pinwheels that spun against her closed lids.

Upstairs, that long-ago afternoon in Hammons Mill, she had bent forward and leaned her upper body against the bed. She shifted her weight slightly; she could no longer feel the knobbly loops of the hooked rug upon which she knelt.

Wait—that was no good, Hattie thought. Maybe if her knees hurt a little bit more, Joey might hurt less! She stood up stiffly, kicked the crudely flowered rug roughly to one side, and then knelt down hard on the bare floor. She lay her cheek against the bumpy white coverlet. Minutes passed.

There was a sudden sharp knock on Hattie's bedroom door. Before she even had a chance to open her mouth, the door swung wide. Hattie struggled stiffly to her feet, numb with cold and fear. Dr. Leavitt looked strange without his cape, she thought dully, like a bird without wings. He looked every bit as helpless as that.

And he was staring at her with pity.

Oh, no, Hattie thought. No. "I call you Dr. Dandy," she heard herself say, her voice hard.

She wanted to hurt that doctor before he could hurt her.

"My dear Miss Harriet," the doctor said, not understanding her words, "I have something difficult to—"

Hattie held out her hands, as if that could stop him. "No," she said, almost conversationally. "Please don't tell me anything more."

Dr. Leavitt lifted his own white hands before him as if mirroring her gesture, but it was as though their weight was unfamiliar to him. "I'm sorry," he said with genuine emotion. "I'm so sorry, my dear."

As if in sympathy with Hattie's rush of memories, Mrs. Spencer's baby started to fill Miss Bulkley's sitting room with his protests. His thin cries brought Hattie back to the present.

Baby Algernon sounded like a kitten, she thought, surprised—what with his mewing and squeaking. His father glared at him, and his mother soothed him. The tiny squall subsided.

"We were thinking that Miss Macintosh may have gone to Manhattan," Miss Brownback said.

"Perhaps shopping," Miss Bulkley added.

"She's not shopping, Miss Bulkley," Miss Patton repeated, earning herself a stern look of rebuke.

But Dominie Spencer's jaw had dropped. "*Manhattan?*" he finally managed to say, as if Miss Brownback had suggested that Fannie might have decided to visit Hell itself. "Then she's lost. His will be done," he added, bowing his head.

"She had quite a lot of money, sir," Hattie objected. "Why, she's probably staying in a fine hotel."

Miss Bulkley stared at Hattie as if she'd forgotten she was still there. "The Dominie didn't mean *that* kind of lost,

Miss Knowlton," she said sharply. "He meant that her soul was lost."

"Oh, surely not," Mrs. Spencer said, horrified. "God would never turn his back on an innocent child. *'His eye is on the sparrow,'* " she quoted. She clasped little Algernon tighter to her bosom as if he, too, might suddenly fly away.

Her husband glared his disapproval, and Hattie knew at once that Mrs. Spencer would pay the price later for her uncharacteristically bold contribution to the conversation.

You were right, Fannie, she thought—a woman *should* use great care in selecting a husband.

"His eye might be on the sparrow," Dominie Spencer said sarcastically, "but I'm certain that He recognizes a lost cause when He sees one."

"Again, not in my Bible!" Miss Patton snapped.

Miss Bulkley was not pleased. "Miss Patton, why don't you and Miss Brownback see to the other girls? You stay," she told Hattie curtly. "You knew her best. You might help us think where she might have gone."

The two teachers exchanged meaningful glances but left the room as directed. Miss Brownback's eyes met Hattie's as she closed the door. *Courage*, she seemed to say.

Miss Bulkley beckoned the Dominie closer to her; he snagged another two triangles of ham sandwich as his hand passed over the plate. He and Miss Bulkley leaned their heads together in muffled conference.

Hattie edged over to where Mrs. Spencer was sitting.

"I'm sure that Fannie will be all right," she told the woman, not knowing why she felt the need to comfort her former neighbor.

Mrs. Spencer shook her head. "I have to tell you, Harriet, that I'm not at all hopeful," she said, keeping her voice low.

"Why not?" Hattie asked, stunned at the woman's words—Mrs. Dominie Spencer, usually so full of chitchat and platitudes!

"Oh, my dear," Mrs. Spencer said sadly, "I don't know. It's just a feeling, that's all. Miss Macintosh was—well, she was so full of life. Too full, perhaps."

"You think Fannie's *dead*?" Hattie's mouth barely managed to form the words.

"Well, perhaps not dead," Mrs. Spencer said, hastening to reassure Hattie. "But in trouble, surely. She's bound to be, a girl like that. So lively-like."

"No!" Hattie said. "Fannie is resourceful and brave and—and—" Her voice faltered.

"She's those things and more, besides," Mrs. Spencer agreed.

"Then why do you say she's in trouble?" Hattie persisted. "You can't know that."

"Not for sure," Mrs. Spencer agreed, almost apologetically. Her troubled face broke into a sudden, unexpected smile. "Do you remember her story about falling out of bed on the train—in her second-best nightgown?" she asked, touching Hattie's arm.

Hattie pressed her lips together hard and nodded. She didn't want to remember stories about Fannie—not yet.

Mrs. Spencer sighed now, the smile wiped off her face. "A girl like that," she repeated, shaking her head.

"Oh, Mrs. Spencer—please don't talk as though Fannie is really *gone*."

Mrs. Spencer looked at her sorrowfully. "Perhaps we'll see her again. I hope we will."

"We *must*," Hattie said.

"But even if we don't," Mrs. Spencer told her, holding up a chapped and reddened hand as if to forestall any objections, "we must always remember her."

"She's not dead," Hattie insisted. In his mother's lap, Algernon began to cry once more.

"I pray not," Mrs. Spencer said simply, rocking her baby. "But at least she *lived*, my dear—and that's more than many of us can say. At least she lived."

SPIDER

attie burst into the bedroom and threw her bag on the rug. It landed with a heavy *thunk*, and dust speckled the air around it. Sophie, Julie, and Mollie were huddled together on Sophie's bed, their hands poised over a half-empty tin of shortbread squares.

"How *could* you?" Hattie said to Sophie, hands on her hips.

Sophie blinked like a china doll. "How could I *what?*" she asked, confused.

"How could you have copied the words from my journal like that?"

Sophie and Julie exchanged a startled look.

"How did you know?" Mollie asked.

"Miss Bulkley showed it to me," Hattie said. "That's what made Fannie run away, Soph. She left it pinned to her blanket so *everyone* would know."

Julie jumped up. "We heard that Fannie left a note, but we didn't know that it was the same—wait here," she said, and she ran from the room.

"I never showed Fannie what you wrote," Sophie said with some spirit. "She was gone when we got back, wasn't she?"

"But you did copy the words out from my journal," Hattie stated, daring her cousin to deny it.

Sophie nodded. "We're *supposed* to share what we write," she said defiantly. "We're the Quartette," she added, as if that sealed her argument.

Hattie could hear her heart beat in her ears. "When did you do it?" she asked.

"Well, your journal fell to the floor," Sophie said evasively. "You know," she added, "that night when Fannie first came. We were arguing about whether or not I could read those funny things you wrote to Jules and Mol." She looked at Mollie, beseeching her for help.

Mollie waved her small hands, as if to say, *Don't involve me in this!*

"We weren't arguing," Hattie said. "I'd already told you *no*. You shouldn't have done that."

"Yes, but—"

Hattie fixed her cousin with a look. "You shouldn't have done that."

Sophie stared at Hattie, seemingly transfixed. "Perhaps not," she finally conceded.

Mollie's jaw sagged; clearly, she was startled at Hattie's victory.

"Don't you ever do such a thing again."

Sophie looked away, blushing.

Julie appeared in the doorway. "It's gone," she said breathlessly. "That piece of paper was right on my desk when we left for Bridgeport, and now it's gone."

"Why didn't you want us to hear what you'd written?" Mollie asked Hattie, genuinely curious.

"As I told Sophie, my journal belongs to me. It's just about my only private possession, in fact—or it *was*," Hattie said, still not taking her eyes off Sophie's face.

Sophie shrugged unconvincingly, as if nothing unusual had just occurred, but her hand was shaking as she smoothed down her skirt. "I never took your journal out of this room—I only copied down some of the words." Then she blushed. "I wanted us to be sisters. You don't think I'm lonely and all, with Mother the way she is? Sisters share things. Besides, I wanted Mollie and Julie to like you."

"We already did," Julie protested. Sophie shrugged. "I put that paper on my desk, and then we forgot all about it, I guess," Julie continued. "I mean, we certainly never showed it to anyone else. It was our own private joke."

"But why did you add those things at the end about how much I hated Fannie?" Hattie asked Sophie. "And you signed my name, too!"

"No, I didn't," Sophie said, indignant. "Never! I—

I don't like Fannie Macintosh much, it's true," she added, looking a little uncomfortable. "But I never wished her ill. Please believe me."

"And Sophie never signed your name, Hattie," Julie said.

"Then—then how did my name get on that piece of paper?" Hattie asked. Now she was confused.

"We don't know," Mollie said, shaking her head.

"Somebody must have put it there," Julie said.

"Well, who else was here over the holiday?" Hattie asked. "Only Fannie."

"One person returned to school before we did," Julie said thoughtfully. "Minnie Bonesteel. She got here on Saturday."

Hattie and Julie stared at one another. "Minnie said she'd get even with Fannie some day," Hattie whispered.

"And she wasn't exactly fond of *you*," Julie added.

"We should go tell Miss Bulkley," Mollie said.

"No," Hattie stated in a tone none of the others dared to argue with. "Fannie Macintosh was my friend. I'll talk to Minnie—alone."

Sophie, Mollie, and Julie blinked at each other in amazement as Hattie swept from the room.

Minnie Bonesteel, Lulu Callender, and Fannie Macintosh were the only three girls at Miss Bulkley's who roomed alone: Minnie, because she was so particular that no one could meet her high—and loudly articulated—standards;

Lulu, because this was simply one more little luxury her papa could buy for her; and Fannie, because the spooky belvedere was the only room available to so late an arrival.

So Hattie guessed that Minnie would be alone in her room.

She hit Minnie Bonesteel's bedroom door three times with the heel of her hand. When there was no answer, she pushed open the door. "I'm coming in," she warned.

Minnie was seated by the window in a black walnut spool-turned chair her parents had sent to the school after Minnie had complained about her room's spartan furnishings. Her skirts were arranged neatly around her ankles, her slippered feet rested flat on the floor, and her red woolen shawl, held secure by Gertrude Spesh's treasured cameo, was wrapped around her shoulders.

She looked like an illustration of ideal young womanhood, Hattie thought angrily—if you didn't know the girl. If you knew her, she was just mean old Minnie Bonesteel, perched like a spider at the corner of her web.

"Well?" Minnie sneered. "Aren't you going to say anything?"

Hattie took a breath; it was amazingly steady, she thought. "I'm going to say quite a lot, really. I was trying to decide where to start, that's all."

Minnie shrugged and stared out the window once more. "I saw you arrive," she said, not turning around. "A *lady* would never have carried her own bag to the door."

"Why are you just sitting there?" Hattie asked, curious

in spite of herself.

"I'm waiting for my poppy," Minnie said.

Hers was the voice with the quaver in it, Hattie thought, surprised. "Why would your father come to Miss Bulkley's now? You only got back on Saturday."

"I wrote him a letter telling him to come get me," Minnie stated. "I'm not staying in this awful place one more minute than I'm absolutely forced to."

"What's the matter?" Hattie asked sarcastically. "Have you run out of people to torment?"

Minnie fingered Gertrude's brooch and glanced in Hattie's direction. "I—I don't know what you're talking about," she said defiantly.

"I'm talking about Fannie Macintosh," Hattie said, "and how you chased her away from Miss Bulkley's."

Minnie smiled a little. "I never chased Fannie away."

"Don't lie!"

Minnie yawned elaborately, patting her mouth daintily as she did so. "I wouldn't bother lying to you, my dear," she told Hattie when she was finished.

Minnie was trying to shift the focus of this fight, Hattie realized, but she couldn't resist a sharp retort. "Don't call me *dear*," she said, echoing the vanished Fannie Macintosh.

Minnie shrugged. "It was a simple courtesy—wasted on you, I see."

More insults, Hattie thought scornfully. "Oh, you're a fine one to talk about courtesy," she cried out. "You, who go prowling through our bedrooms when we're away, then find those stupid words from my journal in Julie's room. You write cruel things at the end and sign my name to them. And, as if that's not bad enough," Hattie added, "you're vicious enough to give the paper to Fannie!"

Minnie looked startled. Aha, Hattie thought.

"How did you know?" Minnie asked, visibly nervous at last.

"That was the note she left," Hattie said flatly.

"Ah," Minnie said, nodding, as if a puzzle had just been solved. "Well, to begin with, I wasn't prowling through your bedrooms—don't flatter yourself."

"Oh, no," Hattie mocked. "You just *happened* to be pawing through the papers on Julie's desk when you found that piece of paper."

"It was right out in the open," Minnie said, "for all the world to see. Fiona was making up the beds in there when I arrived back at school—and she hadn't even finished cleaning *my* room. I went in to have a word with her, and that's when I saw what you wrote."

"So you stole the paper," Hattie stated.

"Call it stealing if you want," Minnie shrugged. "I call it *borrowing*. And then I gave it to Fannie after dinner that night," she added. She tilted her head innocently. "I told her we'd all been passing it around and laughing over it for weeks. I said that everyone had seen it, so she might as well keep it for a souvenir."

"You *didn't*," Hattie said, appalled. But Minnie obviously had. It was exactly the sort of thing she would do.

"Oh, indeed I did," Minnie said, nodding once for emphasis. "As I said before, why would I lie to you? I'm leaving this place for good. Miss Bulkley can do nothing to me now."

"But why did you do it?"

"Because Fannie crossed me," Minnie explained simply, standing up. "And you did, too, *Miss Harriet*—more than once, I might add. So this opportunity was simply too good to pass up."

Hattie took a deep breath. "And you're not the slightest bit sorry for what you've done," she said.

Minnie shrugged again. "Why should I be?" she asked rhetorically. "It serves you and Fannie right. And don't bother repeating any of this to anyone, Hattie, for I'll simply deny every word."

"Poor Fannie," Hattie breathed.

"*'Poor Fannie,'*" Minnie mimicked. "I'm glad she's gone. I hope she never comes back."

"She probably never *will* come back," Hattie said. "And it's all because of you."

Minnie widened her eyes. "I would have said it was because of you, Hattie," she said. "After all, you were the one who put pen to paper."

Hattie thought about this and realized there was a grain of truth to what Minnie had just said. "Well, I never will again," she said, more to herself than to Minnie. It was too dangerous, writing. Better to say what you meant out loud.

"No great loss!"

❦ 23 ❧

"TO HATTIE"

Hattie pushed open the heavy trapdoor and poked her head into the belvedere. There was a full moon, and the room's simple furnishings seemed to be outlined with the light that sifted in through Fannie's thin curtains.

Averting her eyes from the room's now-empty rocking chair and praying silently that it would not move, Hattie climbed the last few stairs slowly. She closed the trapdoor behind her and stood quietly in the center of Fannie's room, hands clasped.

She looked around. There was the advertising poster above Fannie's cot, showing the yellow-haired man cradling his beloved gun.

There were the fancy painted silk pillows, but they were now tossed into every corner of the room as if hurled there by an angry hand.

And there was Fannie's rough blanket—where the note had been left pinned.

Could it all have happened a mere three days ago?

Hattie took a deep breath and gazed around the room once more. It seemed lifeless, she thought, although not much had been taken from it—except for Fannie, of course.

Fannie's clothes still hung on the walls, Hattie noticed. Most of her clothes, anyway, although Hattie knew that Fannie must have taken *some* things with her. Not the brilliant red cape; but then, Fannie would hardly wear such a noticeable garment if she were hoping to slip away unnoticed.

There was the peacock satin waist, too, and the red Balmoral petticoat.

White satin stockings lay tangled in knots on the floor.

And, taking pride of place between the belvedere's two front windows—the same windows Fannie had peeped from when Hattie last turned her back on her—was the glorious *robe de nuit*, shimmering in the moonlight.

It was as though Fannie had left it there especially for Hattie to see.

Drawn to it as if by irresistible force, Hattie crossed the room. She traced her finger along the white-on-white willow-leaf embroidery, remembering her one visit to Fannie's room. How generous Fannie had been, Hattie thought—with her clothes, her candy, and—and her confidences.

Much more generous than she'd been with Fannie,

Hattie admitted to herself. She crushed her face against the robe's thick satin.

Some part of the robe crackled, and Hattie jumped back.

It can't be, she thought, her heart pounding. Every inch of that costly garment was silky, smooth, and soft. She reached out a tentative hand and ran it down the length of the robe.

Another crackle!

Hattie stepped forward and slid her hands down the length of the robe, searching for the source of the noise.

There was something in one of the robe's hidden pockets.

Hardly daring to breathe, Hattie slid her hand into the pocket in question—and pulled out a slightly bulging envelope.

The words *"To Hattie"* were scrawled on the front of the envelope.

There was no letter inside—only the rattles from the littlest snake. *"I don't know why, but they're the worst for poison,"* Fannie had said.

And that's when Hattie thought her heart might break.

MIRROR

r. Macintosh is here!" Mollie said, nearly gasping with excitement as she slipped into Miss Brownback's drawing class moments before the door was to be closed. Fannie Macintosh had been gone for two long weeks, and no word had arrived at school as to her whereabouts.

Mollie placed her hand on her heart and fell back against the wall, panting; she looked rather like a tiny hummingbird pausing in midair for a second, Hattie thought, her own heart pounding every bit as hard as Mollie's must be.

"He's *here?*" Julie asked.

"But there's no noise," Sophie said, cocking her head.

The Quartette paused as one and listened intently, as if expecting frenzied shouts at the very least—and perhaps even carpet-muffled hoofbeats in Miss Bulkley's front hall,

or gunfire!—to announce the arrival of Fannie Macintosh's
father.

Instead, the special hush of a snowy December afternoon filled the small, stuffy room.

"Gladys nearly fainted when he told her his name,"
Mollie reported. "I was just coming down the stairs."

Hattie grabbed her shoulders. "What did he look like?"
she asked, nearly shaking her.

"Was he in fringes and cowboy boots?" Sophie asked.

"Did he have chin whiskers down to his waist, and a
long black whip?" Julie chimed in.

Mollie shook her ringlets and flapped her long eyelashes, bewildered. "He looked quite respectable," she said,
clearly not believing her own words. "He's tall and slim,
and very handsome. But I think he has a *scar*," she added
thrillingly.

"*Who* has a scar?" Miss Brownback's cool voice cut into
the Quartette's interrogation.

"Mr. Macintosh—Fannie's father," Hattie explained.
"He's just arrived."

Everyone within earshot glanced involuntarily at the
door, as if expecting an armed posse to burst into the room,
Hattie thought.

Miss Brownback collected herself first. "Well, that's
excellent news," she announced. "Now, take your seats,
please. We have work to do."

Her students looked a little dashed, but they sat down,

murmuring—until she quelled them with one of her patented looks.

Before their fingers had even been smudged by their skinny sticks of drawing charcoal, however, there was a knock on the classroom door. Fiona poked her head in. "Pardon, miss," she said to Miss Brownback.

"What is it, Fee?" Miss Brownback asked, a little annoyed.

"They want Miss Harriet," Fiona said. "In Miss Bulkley's sitting room."

All faces turned to Hattie, who shrank back in her seat as if she were a plate of ice cream melting on a hot summer's day.

"Poor Hattie," Sophie whispered, and she touched her cousin's hand.

"You'd better go," Miss Brownback said, looking sorry for the girl.

Hattie got to her feet and walked slowly from the room, following Fiona; she dragged her feet as though she was walking through molasses. They were silent until they reached the front hall. "Fee, wait," Hattie said, tugging at the girl's rough sleeve.

Fiona turned around, scared and solemn.

"Does he look sad?" Hattie asked, her heart thudding sickeningly beneath her black-and-gray-striped waist. "Is he *angry?*"

"Well," Fiona said, looking thoughtful, "he weren't crying

or yelling. Not when I left, anyway."

"That's good, isn't it," Hattie said, not letting go of the sleeve. "Don't you think that's a good sign, Fee?"

"I don't know," Fiona said. "Means Miss Fannie's not dead, maybe. But me and Gladys are supposed to go up to her room and pack all her things, so she's not coming back *here*, anyway."

"Wait for a moment," Hattie said, giving the girl's arm a quick squeeze. "I have to go upstairs for a second."

Fiona frowned, alarm showing in her eyes. "You're not going to run away on me too, are you, Miss Harriet? Climb out the window or something daft like that?"

Hattie laughed. "No—nothing daft, I promise, Fee, I'll be right back. Wait here," she repeated, and she ran up the stairs.

The vines, ribbons, and birds depicted in her room's familiar wallpaper seemed suspended in the violet light that poured into the room past the partly drawn green velvet curtains. Outside, big snowflakes fell steadily, cloaking the orderly trees between the house and street until they looked like—like elephants, Hattie thought, smiling in spite of everything.

She never *did* get to tell Fannie about that baby elephant being named for her.

She ran to her desk and slipped a heavy, cream-colored envelope into her pocket. Inside that envelope was the letter it had taken her so long to write.

☞ ☞ ☞

Mr. Macintosh was standing in front of Miss Bulkley's little black fireplace when Hattie entered the room. Miss Bulkley stood near the window, wringing her hands, and Gladys lingered over a tea tray, busying herself so that she need not leave the room and miss whatever was going to happen next.

Fiona went over to assist her.

"Mr. Macintosh, here, as you requested, is Miss Harriet Knowlton," Miss Bulkley said.

He'd asked especially to see her. Hattie blushed, but she stepped resolutely forward and curtsied.

"Hello, my dear," Mr. Macintosh said in a deep, cultivated voice.

He was much as Mollie had described him, Hattie thought, trying not to gape, only even more dashing. There was a small scar that ran along his cheekbone, it was true, looking like a pale line drawn against the darkness of his skin—a rich tone, Hattie knew, that must have resulted from countless hours spent under the western sun.

He was wearing a dark suit that was as fine in its cut and weave as any owned by Uncle Charley, and the only anomaly in his attire was a gold nugget—the size of a pecan!—that hung from his watch chain.

Fannie's father was better even than Heathcote, the best of Miss Woolson's romantic heroes, Hattie thought.

"Miss *Knowlton*," Miss Bulkley was scolding in a reminding way.

"Oh, beg pardon—how do you do," Hattie said.

"Why don't we all sit down?" Mr. Macintosh said, taking charge exactly as if he were the host, rather than Miss Bulkley.

Miss Bulkley perched on a slippery-looking settee, and Hattie sat down gingerly on the edge of a small gilded chair. Mr. Macintosh settled back into his own seat and accepted the cup of tea Gladys offered him—after a brief scuffle with Fiona for the privilege—with a grim smile.

Miss Bulkley waved Gladys and Fiona from the room, then leaned forward and spoke to Hattie. "Mr. Macintosh was telling me that the Pinkerton detectives he had searching for Fannie traced her all the way to New Orleans."

"They *found* her?" Hattie asked, jumping to her feet—but Miss Bulkley gestured for her to sit down again, and so she did.

Clearly in no hurry, Mr. Macintosh sipped some tea, then put the cup down soundlessly on a small piecrust table near to hand. "Yes," he said. "They got there just in time. Another day, and my Fannie would have been either on her way to France or South America. She hadn't quite decided yet. Teach me to be so generous with my girl's allowance," he added, reproaching himself.

"Oh, but *you* didn't know," Miss Bulkley gushed, perhaps thinking a display of sympathy might endear her to him.

The skin around Mr. Macintosh's nostrils seemed to whiten a little, as if he were barely controlling his anger.

Hattie held her breath. "That's right," he said coldly, "I didn't realize how miserable she was here. That was for *you* to tell me, Miss Bulkley. There is such a thing as the U.S. Mail." There was no trace of the west in the man's speech, which made Hattie wonder if Fannie had exaggerated her frontier airs for the girls at Miss Bulkley's.

Miss Bulkley sagged back on the settee, stunned at Mr. Macintosh's harsh words. "But, sir," she said, "I had no way of knowing your daughter was intending any such foolishness. She seemed to be settling in quite well, in fact—wasn't she, Miss Knowlton?"

Hattie cleared her throat and forced herself to look away from Miss Bulkley's imploring gaze. I can be brave *now*, at least, she told herself. "No," she said. "I don't think Fannie was very happy here, Miss Bulkley. I'm sorry to say it."

This time, Miss Bulkley was the one to spring to her feet. "Why, I'm surprised at you!" she scolded, as if Hattie had been the sole cause of Fannie's misery.

Which was not all that far from the truth, Hattie reminded herself.

"Don't you go blaming Miss Knowlton," Mr. Macintosh said, obviously not having any intention of letting this conversation get away from him. "Why, she's the only person here who was kind to my girl! Fannie wrote me all about her, saying she reckoned they were going to be friends one day. That's why I wanted her in the room with us now, to tell her Fannie is all right. Physically, anyway—her spirit is another matter."

Hattie almost cried out, she felt so moved and ashamed.

"*Well*," Miss Bulkley said, drawing herself up in what seemed a parody of dignity, "I thought Fannie simply took it into her head to flee. You know how girls are," she added confidingly, in what appeared to be a remnant of her previous attempt to win the man over.

"I only know my Fannie," Mr. Macintosh said simply. "And I hold you responsible for what happened."

Miss Bulkley wrung her hands as if she were washing them. "Mr. Macintosh," she pleaded, "I'm sure that no judge in the world would—"

"I'm not talking about legal responsibility," Mr. Macintosh interrupted.

The room was silent for a moment. "Miss Bulkley didn't know how unhappy Fannie was," Hattie finally said, steeling herself for what surely would follow.

"Then who *did* know?" Mr. Macintosh asked severely.

Hattie took a deep, shaky breath. "We all did, I suppose," she said. "All us girls."

Miss Bulkley sat up straighter and scowled, not bothering to correct Hattie's grammar. "I'm shocked, Miss Knowlton—shocked."

"Save your outrage, madam," Mr. Macintosh told her dryly. "It wasn't this young girl's responsibility to look out for the well-being of the students here, and I won't have you blaming her unfairly."

Miss Bulkley sagged again.

"But—but what happens next?" Hattie asked after a moment.

Mr. Macintosh gave her a brief wintry smile. "I gather Fannie's things together and join her in New Orleans, Miss Knowlton. And when I get there, why, I intend to let her know that she's not quite so alone in the world as she seems to think."

Hattie's eyes filled with tears, and without even a glance in Miss Bulkley's direction, she handed Mr. Macintosh the envelope she'd gotten from her room. "Give Fannie this, will you?" she asked.

She had written in immaculate style, straight from *The Lady's Guide to Perfect Gentility*:

My dear friend,

If you receive this letter, it means that you are safe and well, for which fact I am profoundly thankful. We have all been so worried about you, Fannie, but I most especially, as I cannot help but feel responsible for the great unhappiness that caused you to run away.

Minnie Bonesteel added those last hateful words to what I wrote, and then she signed my name to them. Also, Minnie lied to you when she said all the girls had read those words. Only Sophie, Julie, and Mollie read what I wrote, although I didn't know they had.

Minnie is gone now, but that is scant comfort to me.

Fannie, when I wrote those mocking words about you in my

journal, it was before I came to know you. Please believe me. As to why I wrote them, well, I think I was just flapping my gums, as Miss Pat sometimes accuses us girls of doing when we chatter. Only I did it on paper, and I'm sorry.

You were right to leave me the little rattle, Fannie. I will keep it always, and I hope it reminds me to guard my tongue—or pen!—whenever poisonous words might tempt me.

I apologize, too, for turning away from you when you tried to be my friend. That was an error I will always regret.

Finally, I apologize for turning my back on you that last day. I was a coward to do it, and I regret it more mightily than you could ever guess.

When I stand at the mirror now, I see a girl who is perhaps a little bit wiser and a little bit kinder. I do not deserve your friendship, but if you were here, Fannie Macintosh, by gosh, I would try to earn it.

You are the bravest girl I ever met. I plan to be braver from now on, too. Believe me to be,

Yours most sincerely,

Hattie

Mr. Macintosh slipped the envelope into his pocket. "I wish you could give her this yourself, my dear," he said. "I know it will mean a lot to my girl. But perhaps you will see her again some day."

Hattie smiled. "Maybe some day," she agreed. "I have my hopes."

Hattie Knowlton, around age 18

POSTSCRIPT

Hattie Knowlton was my great-grandmother.

When my grandmother—Hattie's daughter—died, she was a very old lady in her nineties. In clearing out her desk, I came upon a small notebook that was the journal her mother had kept during the last months of 1882, while she was a student at Miss Bulkley's Seminary, in Tarrytown, New York. "Seminary" was the title given to many girls' schools of that time; such designation had little to do with religion.

It is this journal—the one described in Chapter 7—that inspired this book. The journal itself is an amusing account of Hattie and her fellow students, filled with the puns and word play that were so popular then. Clearly, such journals were to be read aloud as entertainment.

Tucked away at the back of the notebook, however, was a letter that made Hattie's lighthearted writing more poignant. Written to my grandmother in 1945, more than sixty years after Hattie wrote her last word in the journal, the letter was from Mrs. E. L. Pupke, the former Julie Wilcox, Hattie's friend and a member of "the Quartette." It said:

> *When Hat's mother died leaving her with little Joe, her aunt came to live with them until Joe died. After Joe's death it*

was not long before the Aunt died. Then Hat was alone.

Uncle Charley then "took over" and they decided the best plan was for her to stay at school until something could be arranged . . .

Given that Julie was writing this to Hattie's daughter, it seemed that the chronology of events might have been news to my grandmother, indicating that Hattie had told her daughter as little of that sad time in her life as was included in the journal. This might seem strange to us today, but those were different times.

The 1880s was a decade of great excitement and contradiction. People were simultaneously enchanted by the idea of the American West, for instance, and drawn toward anything European.

Established religions in the 1880s were very influential. However, they competed not only with each other and with new religions, but with Utopian communities, health movements, mysticism, and outright—if usually concealed—disbelief. In my novel, Hattie experiences some of the religious turmoil of the era. She shockingly confides that she thinks ". . . God isn't worth shucks," even as she obediently trots off to church each Sunday.

Many of America's great fortunes were made in the years following the Civil War, but prosperity was by no means assured to everyone. The difference between the few rich people and the many poor ones was vast, although the middle class was growing, thanks in part to America's thriving industries.

Snobbery was rampant.

On a more individual level, however, people were different in some important ways from the way we are today. "Sharing" personal misfortune was not at all common then; in fact, reticence was a virtue. And pride was still a sin.

All the first names in the journal are as Hattie wrote them. The only name fabrication is Mollie's last name, which Hattie never mentioned. I changed the girls' ages and the order of deaths in Hattie's family very slightly. There was no need to make up any of the major characters, however, because Hattie gave them all to me. The journal entries are all Hattie's own.

The newspaper clipping quoted in the novel is almost exactly as it appeared in print. (A great-great-grandfather of mine, by the way, was P. T. Barnum's next-door neighbor in Seaside Park; my father told me the story of Mr. Barnum's exotic animals mowing the lawns, a tale that a by-then-ancient gardener told him.)

The one thing missing from Hattie's journal, as from most journals, was a plot, and so I invented one. A plot needs a villain or two, and I selected these from the list of characters Hattie provided. If in so doing I have wronged anyone, however long gone, I apologize; I view all of the people Hattie wrote about with fondness and respect—as, indeed, she seemed to.

I apologize especially to Minnie Bonesteel, who from all accounts was never anything other than a good friend to Hattie.

As far as I know, Hattie wrote nothing similar to this journal—or, indeed, anything at all of substance—for the rest of her life. This is sad, as I think she was a wonderful writer.

What happened next in Hattie's life? Harriet Knowlton married Friend William Smith, the son of Bridgeport's postmaster, after she finished her studies at Miss Bulkley's Seminary. They settled in Bridgeport, Connecticut, probably to Hattie's delight.

As a boy, Friend William Smith—known to me as "Grandpa Smith," although he died before I was born—shook hands with President Abraham Lincoln.

Years later, according to his own brief (and modest) account of his life, he crawled across the Brooklyn Bridge while the bridge was being built at the request of someone from the New York Telephone Company, carrying a wire reel on his back. "By means of this wire the first telephone message was sent from New York to Brooklyn," he wrote.

In his professional life, Grandpa Smith was a patent attorney, working, for instance, with Thomas Edison at Menlo Park for six months. Grandpa Smith also wrote that he was the first person to sing over the telephone.

Hattie died in 1928, at the age of 65, after having been ill for many years. Grandpa Smith died shortly after the start of World War II. Both are buried in the Sleepy Hollow Cemetery in Tarrytown, near Hattie's little brother, Jotham.

Hattie and Grandpa Smith had three children: one son and two daughters. Hattie named her daughters Sophie and Julie, after Sophie Hubbard and Julie Wilcox, thereby revealing how close she felt to her friends from Miss Bulkley's.

My great-aunt Sophie Smith never married. She was very adventurous; she drove an ambulance for the Red Cross in France during World War I. After the war, Sophie worked with friends to raise funds for French children orphaned by the war. In addition, she was among the first—if not *the* first—to bring early French films to the United States, opening a small cinema in Greenwich Village.

My grandmother Julie Wilcox Smith loved France, too, attending an art school for young ladies in Paris in 1911, the year before her marriage. Her fiancé attended Yale as her father had done; he fought in France during World War I but never wanted to return to that country, having found the war so terrible. And so they never did.

Julie Smith married DeVer Cady Warner in 1912. Julie and DeVer Warner had three sons and one daughter, who died shortly after her birth. One of their sons was my father, Stuart Todd Warner.

Stuart Warner married Mary Jane Whiteman in 1936, and I am one of their three children.